AF432386

Snow Toys for You

Alaska Cozy Mystery
Book 13

Wendy Meadows

Copyright © 2024 by Wendy Meadows

All rights reserved.

No portion of this book may be reproduced in any form without written permission from the publisher or author, except as permitted by U.S. copyright law.

This publication is designed to provide accurate and authoritative information in regard to the subject matter covered. It is sold with the understanding that neither the author nor the publisher is engaged in rendering legal, investment, accounting or other professional services. While the publisher and author have used their best efforts in preparing this book, they make no representations or warranties with respect to the accuracy or completeness of the contents of this book and specifically disclaim any implied warranties of merchantability or fitness for a particular purpose. No warranty may be created or extended by sales representatives or written sales materials. The advice and strategies contained herein may not be suitable for your situation. You should consult with a professional when appropriate. Neither the publisher nor the author shall be liable for any loss of profit or any other commercial damages, including but not limited to special, incidental, consequential, personal, or other damages.

Chapter One

Sarah drove a bright red Dodge Journey down a snowy street lined with middle class houses with brick chimneys tossing sweet-smelling smoke up into a icy-gray sky. Each house sat in a square pond of snow that would turn into a lush green lawn when summer arrived; skateboards, bicycles, footballs, and other outdoor items lay hidden under the heavy snow like secret treasures waiting to be unearthed. Bare, skeletal trees that would bloom back to life when spring arrived stood over the houses like sad voices whispering through a single winter tear—or maybe that was only Sarah's imagination tossing that bit of pale spice into the mix? Sarah wasn't exactly thrilled to be visiting her cousin Bonnie, and she wasn't thrilled to be in the state of Michigan, either...Michigan was far away from Alaska, and Conrad was in Alaska. "We're looking for 984 Autumn Bridge Road," she told Amanda in a bland voice.

Amanda nodded, continued to munch on a Chick-fil-A chicken biscuit she was holding, and made a muffled sound with her mouth that might have meant, "Got it." Sarah sighed. Amanda's version of "got it" was extra Chick-fil-A sauce. "Oh...there...there!" Amanda suddenly cried, nearly gushing bites of food out of her mouth and onto her green coat. Amanda pointed at a barn-shaped mailbox.

Sarah eased the SUV to a stop and checked the address printed on the side of the farmhouse mailbox. "Nine eight four," she read the numbers aloud, confirming, and then looked at the two-story white and brown Bavarian-style house at the end of a driveway that had been recently plowed. A blue 1967 convertible Volkswagen sat at the end of the driveway facing a two-car garage. "I guess Cousin Bonnie has been out this morning?" she asked and—reluctantly—pulled the SUV into the driveway and parked behind the Volkswagen. "As if solving a difficult murder case in London wasn't enough...now I have to visit Cousin Bonnie...of all things," Sarah complained to Amanda.

Amanda munched down on her biscuit and then pawed through the Chick-fil-A bag on her lap in search of any stray hash browns. "I had fun in London," she smiled.

"Of course, you had fun...you weren't the one who had to catch a killer. Pete and I got stuck with that task." Sarah locked her eyes on the two-car garage and then studied the blue Volkswagen. "Well, at least you got to spend time with your husband," she told Amanda, struggling to sound somewhat positive.

Amanda fished some hash browns out of the bag, scarfed them down, and then picked up her hot coffee from the cup holder between the seats. "Love, my hubby and I had a lovely time," she said, taking down some of the coffee, "but the real fun came when he took me on all those shopping trips. That bloke knows how to make his wife happy. But, that said, I am sorry you and Pete had such a difficult time. I'm sorry Conrad nearly broke his ankle, too. Poor bloke had to sit in the hotel the entire trip and read."

"While Pete and I chased a crazy killer all over London...in the freezing rain, I might add," Sarah pointed out. "But who gets sick? Conrad...the one who sat in a warm hotel room through the entire trip."

Amanda grinned. Sarah was being cranky. "Poor baby."

Sarah looked at Amanda, saw her best friend grinning at her, and then let out a tired laugh. "Oh, I'm sorry, June Bug. I don't mean to be so fussy. I wanted to spend time with Conrad after all that, but instead here we are, sitting in Cousin Bonnie's driveway." Sarah let her eyes search the white world outside the SUV. "Cousin Bonnie...well, she's...different," Sarah said in a pained voice.

"Love, you told me your cousin was a bit odd before we left Alaska," Amanda said and polished off her coffee. "You've had a gray cloud over your head ever since we drove away from your cabin." Amanda tossed the empty coffee cup into the paper bag sitting on her lap and studied the house. "Looks like a nice house...normal neighborhood...even the car looks cool. I don't see a problem. Why so gloomy? Your cousin called and asked to see you and here we are...no big deal, right?"

Sarah glanced down at the brown coat she wore over her gray dress. "Amanda...the only reason I agreed to make this trip is because of my mother," she explained. "My mother was always very fond of Cousin Bonnie."

"And the reason being...?" Amanda dared to ask.

Sarah kept her eyes low. "Cousin Bonnie...made her...laugh."

"Laugh?" Amanda asked and looked at Sarah as if the

woman had gone mad. "Oh my...that's utterly dreadful. Please, take us from this terrible place before we are swallowed up by a never-ending horror!" she begged and began scratching at the windshield. "Oh please, save me from the woman who made your mother...laugh!"

"Very funny, June Bug." Sarah rolled her eyes. "I don't expect you to understand."

Amanda made a silly face at Sarah. "You're being a tad...shall I dare say...childish? Why so secretive about her? You really haven't told me much about Bonnie Malloy other than she's a divorcee who owns a toy shop. And," Amanda added, "you haven't told me why Bonnie asked you to visit her? Now, being your one and only best friend in the whole wide world, I know better than to pick at your mind when you're all tangled up. But love, don't you think the time has arrived to untangle the knots in your mind and talk to me?"

Sarah raised her eyes and searched for signs of human movement. Surely Bonnie had heard the SUV arrive? "June Bug, years back, when I was in my early twenties...Bonnie...well, she saved my life."

"Oh?" Amanda raised an eyebrow and waited for the goods. She grabbed a few more hash browns, dipped them in Chick-Fil-A sauce, and waited for the show to begin. "Do tell."

Sarah looked at Amanda's expression and fought the urge to roll her eyes again. "We were swimming at the beach. I got caught in a riptide current...there were no lifeguards around...and Bonnie swam out and saved me. It's that simple, June Bug."

"But?" Amanda added in a juicy voice.

"But," Sarah added and let out a heavy sigh, "Bonnie never

let me live that day down. She always reminded me...over and over...of the fact that she saved me from a watery death...and to make it worse, my mother"—Sarah rubbed her eyes and made a pained face—"always applauded Bonnie's...'heroic deed.' With that said, June Bug, my mother made me promise to repay Bonnie any way I could if the situation ever arose."

"Oh...I see," Amanda blurted out. "Bonnie Malloy called Alaska and told you it was time to pay up or shut up, right?"

"Cousin Bonnie called me and asked me for a favor. She didn't say what...but she did remind me that I owed her for saving my life." Sarah searched the snow with weary eyes. "June Bug, Cousin Bonnie...well, she..."

"What?" Amanda begged.

"She's not a horrible person," Bonnie struggled to explain. "Cousin Bonnie was never aware that she rubbed it in my face so badly, the fact that she saved my life. She...well, she's... different, but not really in a bad way...just...in a way that can drive a normal person insane."

Before Amanda could respond, a white wooden door next to the garage opened up and a large, plump woman wearing a red ski coat and blue ski pants burst out like a fierce linebacker. "Cousin Sarah!" the woman yelled, slapped a red muffler hat down over a mess of red and pink curly hair, and hurried toward the SUV.

"Oh my," Amanda whispered.

"Told you so," Sarah grimaced and reluctantly stepped out of the SUV. Seconds later Bonnie Malloy swopped Sarah up off her feet and began spinning her around and around. "Hello, Cousin Bonnie...how...are you?" Sarah asked as her world became a white blur.

"It's been years," Bonnie cried out in a voice swooping

with eager joy, more the voice of a ten-year-old than that of a woman in her forties. "Oh, it's so wonderful to see you!"

Amanda eased out of the SUV, watched Bonnie spin Sarah around and around, and tried to decide whether to run or help her tortured friend. "Uh...hello," Amanda called out. "I'm Amanda—"

Bonnie let go of Sarah so quick that the poor woman lost her footing, stumbled backward, and landed in a pile of shoveled snow. "Amanda Hardcastle!" Bonnie let out a whoop of joy, hightailed it over to Amanda, and grabbed the woman before she could run. "Give Bonnie a hug!"

"I...just...ate...oh my!" Amanda cried out as Bonnie picked her up and began swinging her around and around. "It's...nice to...meet you...too," she cried.

Sarah rubbed her back, scrambled to her feet, and hurried over to Bonnie. "Uh...maybe we can go inside and have some coffee?" she suggested and placed a gentle hand on Bonnie's shoulder.

Bonnie dropped Amanda and spun around to face Sarah, eyes glowing with excitement and an innocent face consumed with absolute joy. Poor Amanda went flying backward and ended up on her butt in a pile of snow. "Coffee, yeah, sure. I made a pot of coffee. Come on." Bonnie grabbed Sarah's arm and dragged her toward the house, Amanda scrambling to her feet to join them, though trying to stay at a safe distance.

Once inside, Bonnie pulled Sarah into a kitchen that never left the 1950s. The walls were papered in a brown, flowered wallpaper that had seen better days, with green cabinets and a green and white-checkered linoleum that time had forgotten. "I also made a batch of peppermint cupcakes. My specialty," Bonnie announced in a proud voice, bustling over to the counter and dropping a messy pile of gloves, scarf, and parka along the way. Puddles of melting snow began to accumulate wherever Bonnie walked, falling off her boots and out of her crazy red and pink curls. "You like cupcakes, right?"

"Oh...sounds nice," Sarah replied and carefully eased over to a round table with a red and white tablecloth and sat down. As she did, Amanda eased her head through the doorway, spotted Bonnie busy at the coffee pot, and made a wild dash for the kitchen table.

Bonnie clapped her hands. "Oh, this is so wonderful," she nearly cried. "I went to Mr. Cunningham's grocery store earlier and got more coffee...milk...bread...and a whole bunch of goodies." Bonnie walked to the door and closed it and then tossed her snow pants onto a hook. She looked at Sarah and Amanda with a simple, staring joy, rather like a Winnie the Pooh gazing at Piglet or Rabbit. "How do you girls like your coffee? I like my coffee with lots and lots of creamer and a tad bit of sugar."

Amanda couldn't take her eyes off Bonnie. When Sarah had mentioned that her cousin was different, the label "odd" landed in Amanda's mind. But now Amanda fully understood what Sarah's version of "different" meant. "Uh...cream and sugar, yes, love, that sounds nice."

"Oh, I just love your little accent," Bonnie told Amanda and clapped her hands like a young schoolgirl, forgetting all about the coffee pot. "Oh, it's so quaint...so neat."

"Amanda is from London," Sarah explained, hoping to calm Bonnie down.

"You don't say?" Bonnie gushed. "My...London. It must be nice to be from a land famous for its chocolate."

"What? No, I think you're referring to..." Amanda bit down on her tongue. "Yes...chocolate."

Bonnie clapped her hands, retrieved three red and white coffee cups, filled them with steaming hot coffee, and then hurried off to gather up a tall plastic canister full of powdered creamer and a red and white sugar bowl. "Here we are," she smiled, setting everything on the table.

Sarah shot Amanda a guilty eye. "She's so sweet," she whispered as Bonnie hurried off to get the cream and sugar, "but—"

"I understand, love," Amanda whispered back.

Bonnie hurried back to the kitchen table and sat down across from Sarah. "How do you like what I've done with the kitchen?" she asked in an excited voice.

Sarah and Amanda glanced around the kitchen. Except for peppermint-striped curtains hanging over the kitchen sink— horribly clashing but somehow normal—the kitchen appeared old and vintage. "Uh...nice," Sarah told Bonnie.

"I replaced the knobs on all the cabinets," Bonnie said in a sneaky voice. "The old knobs were metal...I put on new wooden knobs and painted them all brown."

Amanda let her eyes search all the knobs attached to the kitchen cabinets. "Nice," she told Bonnie and then decided to try and relax. "May I have some sugar and cream, please?"

"Why, of course," Bonnie told Amanda and then made a confused face. "Wait...I forgot...oh yes...dear me." Bonnie exploded to her feet, went over to a kitchen drawer, snatched out a silver spoon, retrieved a red and white saucer, and ran back to the table. "Sometimes I would forget my head if it weren't attached," she joked, with a slight nervous giggle. "I don't get guests very often."

Amanda felt pity rise in her heart. She looked at Sarah with sad eyes and then simply reached over the table and patted the woman's hand. "You're doing just fine, love," she promised.

Sarah heard the compassion in Amanda's voice and then felt guilt strike her heart. "Yes, Cousin Bonnie, no need to apologize. We all forget, at times," she said and then decided to throw in a compliment. "I do like the new knobs. Very nice."

Bonnie blushed. "Oh…it wasn't much," she told Sarah and then remembered the hat covering her head and laughed. "My, I'm such a forgetful ninny this morning," she said and snatched the muffler hat off her head.

Sarah smiled, looked down at her coffee, and decided to take a sip. To her shock the coffee was absolutely delicious—as a matter of fact, the coffee tasted better than any coffee she had ever tasted in her life. "My, this coffee is delicious," she told Bonnie.

"I pay a dollar and ninety cents extra for the good brand," Bonnie confessed, giggled, and then filled her coffee with heaps of powdered creamer. "Oh, this is so wonderful," she nearly sang. She looked pleased as punch to have two visitors. After a moment, Sarah realized something.

Sarah gave Amanda a confused eye. "Uh, Cousin Bonnie…if it's okay to ask, why did you ask me to visit you in Michigan?"

"Yes, love, why the reason for a family gathering?" Amanda inquired.

Bonnie raised her wide eyes and looked at Amanda. "I saved her life, you know," she told Amanda and tossed a thumb at Sarah. "A gal can't forget such a thing."

"Yes, I told Amanda how you saved my life," Sarah explained to Bonnie.

Bonnie went back to filling her coffee cup with creamer, stirring it idly. "There comes a time when you need someone who can do you a favor," she said in a voice that quickly lost its joy—like a hot kitchen suddenly being opened up to the frigid, frosty morning. "I saved your life, Cousin Sarah...swam right out into the ocean to get you."

"Yes, you did," Sarah nodded and watched a dark cloud cross Bonnie's sunny features.

Bonnie picked up the silver spoon she had brought to the table and began stirring her coffee. "Saved your life...now maybe you can return the favor," she said in a solemn voice that made Sarah and Amanda look at each other with worried eyes.

Chapter Two

Bonnie stirred her fragrant coffee with a smile, but all of a sudden, the good coffee and the prospect of guests in her house wasn't enough. The joy inside her vanished as suddenly as sunshine disappearing behind an ugly, dark cloud. She felt a deep, furious anger ignite inside of her heart. "I saved your life!" she yelled at Sarah, slapped the table with her large right hand, nearly spilling her coffee, and then simply shook her head. "A gal can't forget such a thing...and now I need a favor."

Amanda grabbed Sarah's hand. "Love, maybe we should—"

Sarah watched Bonnie's eyes. The black cloud that had formed at record pace dissipated just as quickly. "Cousin Bonnie?" she asked in a careful voice.

Bonnie felt a strange tingling in her mind. Then she felt her smile return and a contented excitement entered her heart. "Oh my...oh dear...did I have another episode?" she asked and then giggled like a schoolgirl who had accidentally burped loudly in a silent classroom. "My, oh my..."

Amanda gave Sarah a deeply worried look. "Bonnie love, should we call someone?"

"Nah," Bonnie told Amanda and went back to her coffee with a happy smile. "My psychiatrist says I suffer from mood swings. Something about how...people treat me like I'm stupid...and this deep anger builds up inside of me and kinda pops out from time to time like a steam pipe forming a small crack under pressure."

"Oh...well...I guess you would know best, love," Amanda replied, desperately trying to speak in a way that would make Bonnie appear like the woman was a genius. "A woman knows her own mind."

Bonnie took a sip of her coffee. "Indeed," she smiled. "That's why I made cupcakes before you arrived...a whole batch of my famous peppermint cupcakes."

"The cupcakes sound delicious, Cousin Bonnie," Sarah spoke, maintaining a calm voice. "Before we eat any cupcakes, maybe you can tell me how I can repay you for saving my life? You said you needed a favor?"

"Oh yes," Bonnie said and nodded up and down, up and down, so much that Amanda became dizzy.

"Love...what's the favor?" Amanda begged, grabbed Bonnie's hand, and forced a dizzy smile to her face. "Please..."

Bonnie lowered her eyes and glanced around the kitchen as if she were surrounded by a den of secret spies. "Well," she said and dropped her voice down into a secretive whisper, "someone has been sending me real mean letters. I've been finding those letters slid under the door of my toy store...real mean letters...real mean, oh yes, real mean."

"What do the letters say?" Sarah asked, feeling alarm wander into her mind.

"Well," Bonnie said, glanced around the kitchen at all the invisible spies her mind was seeing, and continued, "each letter has the same message typed out." Bonnie lowered her voice even more. "Each letter says 'Leave or Die. You have one month.' Well, I got my first letter close to a month ago. As a matter of fact, four days from today will make an exact month. Creepy, huh?"

Amanda glanced at Sarah. Sarah focused on Bonnie with worried eyes. "Honey, why didn't you contact me earlier?" she asked in a desperate voice. "Why did you wait so long?"

"Because," Bonnie replied as if Sarah were insane, "it ain't right to ask for a favor if it's for nothing. At first, I thought it was just some kids pulling a prank. No need to call out the cavalry." Bonnie lifted her eyes, searched the kitchen, saw all the invisible spies vanish into thin air, and then giggled. "Besides, I've been dating a new man," she said in an excited voice, grabbed Sarah's and Amanda's hands, squeezed so tight that both women grimaced in pain, and then giggled. "His name is José Lopez."

"José Lopez?" Sarah asked in a pained voice, trying to pull her hand free.

"José arrived at my toy store the same day I received my first mean letter," Bonnie explained, let go of Sarah's and Amanda's hands, and took a sip of coffee. "Ooh, this needs more cream."

Sarah rubbed her hand and watched Bonnie grab the powder creamer and go at it. "Cousin Bonnie, who is this José Lopez?"

"Oh, he's so handsome," Bonnie blushed and then giggled. "José is so sweet...oh, he's a little bit older than me, but that's okay. My daddy was seven years older than momma, remember, Cousin Sarah?"

"I remember," Sarah replied and offered Bonnie a soft smile that hid the beginnings of a very painful headache. "Cousin Bonnie, can you tell me more about José Lopez?"

Bonnie put down the coffee creamer, blushed, tucked her head low, and then said, "I think José wants to marry me."

Amanda gave Sarah a look. "So quickly? What do you know about him, or his family?" Bonnie seemed lost, unable to answer the question. "Love, where does José work?" she tried gently. Upsetting Bonnie Malloy was the last thing in the world Amanda wanted to do.

"Oh, José never talks about his work," Bonnie explained and tested her coffee with another sip. "Ah, perfect."

Sarah took a sip of her coffee and stared at Bonnie. Bonnie had four days to either leave her toy store or die; and a new boyfriend, by some crazy coincidence. "Cousin Bonnie, can I see the letters you've been receiving?"

"Oh sure!" Bonnie bounced up to her feet, slipped a little on one of the melted snow puddles on the kitchen floor, and slid to a stop at the refrigerator. She yanked open the freezer door and pulled out a plastic bag holding a bunch of folded papers. "I put the letters in the freezer...no one ever thinks about looking into the freezer," she said in a proud voice.

"Very smart," Amanda complimented Bonnie. Bonnie blushed and grinned from ear to ear. "No really, love, you're a very clever woman."

"Oh, I should've known you'd be sweet. Sweet because you come from the land where they make chocolate so sweet," Bonnie gushed, running to Amanda and hugging the woman.

"Oh, I...thank you...and...I need air...please...air..." Amanda begged.

Bonnie let go of Amanda. "So sweet...love your accent," she said and then, without any warning, tossed the frozen bag of letters at Sarah. "Hot potato!" she laughed.

Sarah managed to catch the bag of letters and forced a smile to her lips. "Hot potato...caught it," she struggled to laugh back.

Bonnie patted Sarah's shoulder. "Okay, you're a cop...that's why I asked you to come and help me. You were the only relative that made sense to ask for help...so...do your cop stuff," she told Sarah and forced a serious look into her eyes. She sat down and waited patiently for Sarah to get to work. "I won't make a peep...everybody be quiet...no sound...hush..."

"Uh...thank you," Sara told Bonnie and carefully began to investigate the frozen letters. Amanda decided to drink her coffee and wait. As silence consumed the kitchen air, Bonnie began to hum the theme song to *Inspector Gadget*, grinning a little.

Sarah raised her head, looked at Bonnie, saw the woman staring at her with anxious eyes as she hummed, and then went back to work. "Well," Sarah said and closed the plastic bag holding the letters, "all the letters are identical and relay the same message."

"I done told you that," Bonnie said and gave Sarah a curious eye. "You are a cop, right, Cousin Sarah? I mean, I didn't go and make a mistake calling you, did I?"

"I'm a retired cop," Sarah pointed out, "but a cop all the same." Bonnie handed Amanda the bag of letters. "All the letters are printed on computer paper. They're even typed in the same font and size. Looks like Arial, size 12 font."

"Sarah's a writer...she knows the facts," Amanda assured Bonnie and began to investigate the letters herself. "My, these are mean letters."

"I already told you that," Bonnie told Amanda and rolled her eyes at Sarah. "She sure is sweet but not very bright."

"Hey!" Amanda objected and then caught her tongue. "Uh, I'm just confirming what Sarah said," she told Bonnie, winced, and quickly ducked her eyes back down to the letter she was holding.

Sarah took a sip of her coffee. "Cousin Bonnie, the letters don't actually give me a lot of clues. I want to know more about José Lopez."

"Oh...golly," Bonnie blushed, "José sure likes me. He told me he liked me last night at dinner." Bonnie lowered her voice. "I cooked us Chinese food...a bit dangerous," she giggled. "Chinese food gives me gas, but José just loves sweet and sour chicken."

"Uh, Cousin Bonnie, why did José visit your toy store, that first time you met?" Sarah asked, remaining cautious in her questioning.

Bonnie's face beamed. "José collects model cars," she explained in a happy voice. "And I just so happen to sell model car kits at my store. As a matter of fact, my toy store sells model car kits along with model airplane and model house kits. Vintage Toys...that's my store. I sell toys from the good old days, toys that last." Bonnie wrinkled her nose as if she caught a whiff of something sour. "The toys people make today are garbage."

"Tell me about it," Amanda quickly agreed before she

could catch her tongue. "I mean...all plastic and no substance. Toys made today are not the quality of toys from my childhood."

"See? She gets it," Bonnie nodded emphatically. "Do you remember the old Atari you had, Cousin Sarah?" Bonnie asked in an excited voice. Sarah nodded. "I remember that us kids used to sit around for hours playing Asteroids and Centipede." Bonnie drained her coffee as her eyes glowed with sweet memories. "I remember when my daddy bought me my first Nintendo...oh, I played Mario Brothers for hours and hours...and do you know until this very day I still can't save the princess?" Bonnie rolled her eyes. "I get lost in the drainpipes when I arrive at the last level...stupid drainpipes..."

Sarah took a sip of coffee and waited for Bonnie to quit fussing about an old Nintendo game. As she waited, her own mind traveled back through time and saw a young Sarah Garland in her mother's living room in front of an old television, jumping on mushrooms and turtles while trying to help Mario save the princess. It had been years since Sarah had visited that memory...years since she had allowed her adult mind to entertain the joy the child she had once been had enjoyed so much. "Those were sweet days," she whispered.

"They sure were," Bonnie sighed and then exclaimed, "Say, why not play?"

"Play...what?" Sarah dared to ask.

"I have my Nintendo upstairs in my game room...I have Mario Brothers 1, 2 and 3...I have Contra...Paper Boy...Karate Kid...all the classics. Let's go upstairs and play!"

"Uh...maybe later," Sarah told Bonnie and pointed at the bag of letters. "Honey, we have four days to figure out who sent you those letters."

"Oh...yeah, I guess you're right," Bonnie agreed and shook her head. "I guess I wasn't being very smart. My psychiatrist tells me that sometimes I'm not very...what was the word she used...oh yeah...practical. I don't mean to be that way, I just get so excited is all."

Amanda felt pity for Bonnie. "Love, I have a question."

"Yes?"

"Haven't these letters worried you in the least bit?" Amanda asked.

Sarah waited for Bonnie to reply. She saw the woman's eyes slowly fill with a mixture of worry and hope. "Well, I was really scared at first but then...well," she said and blushed, "José walked into my life. It's hard to stay scared when you're falling in love with a man like Jose...he's just so unlike my last husband." Bonnie's eyes quickly turned dark. "That lousy, good-for-nothing bum!" she yelled and struck the kitchen table with a furious fist. "I worked...he played golf...I made money...he spent it..."

Amanda quickly scooted her chair over, grabbed Sarah's hand, and waited for the storm to pass. "It's...alright, love...calm down...please."

Bonnie threw her eyes at Amanda. "Calm down?" she blazed and then, without any notice, the dark storm vanished from her eyes like a balloon popping. "Oh dear...another episode, I'm afraid."

Amanda made a mental note to never mention Bonnie's ex-husband. Sarah did the same. "Honey, tell me more about —" Sarah stopped when the telephone on the kitchen counter began to ring.

"Oh, that might be José," Bonnie exclaimed like a woman rolling around in piles of rose petals and diamonds. She shot to her feet and ran across the kitchen. "Hello, José...José ?" she asked in an excited voice. "Oh...you're not José...who is this?" she asked as a frown formed on her face.

Sarah gave Amanda a worried eye, stood up, and walked over to Bonnie. "Who is on the phone, Cousin Bonnie?" she asked.

Bonnie's frown deepened. "Oh...I see...well, uh...here..." Bonnie slammed the phone into Sarah's hands, burst into tears, and stormed out of the kitchen.

"Oh dear," Amanda gasped and began to stand up.

"Better stay with me," Sarah warned her best friend and then focused on the phone call. "Yes, this is Sarah Garland...I mean Spencer. Who am I speaking to, please?"

"This is Detective Tony Massio," a man spoke in a thick accent that sounded more Italian than American. "Are you the cop Ms. Malloy told me she called down from Alaska?"

"I'm Bonnie's cousin, yes," Sarah confirmed.

"Aren't you the cop who caught the Back Alley Killer?" Tony asked in a curious voice, turning away from the dead body in the back storeroom of Bonnie's toy store.

"I...well, before I retired I handled many difficult cases when I lived in Los Angeles, yes," Sarah explained. "Detective Massio, what is this all about?"

"A murder," Tony declared. "I'm standing over the body of José Lopez as we speak."

Sarah's stomach dropped. She turned her head and looked at Amanda. "José Lopez is dead," she whispered.

"Oh my," Amanda said in a scared voice and looked toward the kitchen door. "Oh, that poor dear."

"Detective Massio—"

"Call me Tony," the man insisted. Sarah could hear him

walking carefully through the crime scene. "Someone put a knife in José's back."

"Detective...Tony...my cousin is—"

"Is the number one person of interest," Tony interrupted Sarah. "I searched Jose's coat pockets and found a letter on him. It matches the letters Bonnie claims someone has been sending her for the past month. She has some answering to do." Tony reached into the pocket of his long gray trench coat and fished out a cheap cigar. He fancied himself a suave detective—a little dangerous, a little hip—but his chubby face, scraggly black mustache, and messy black hair told another story. "I'm afraid I'm going to have to bring Bonnie Malloy downtown for questioning."

Sarah nodded. "Of course. I'll drive Bonnie to your office personally. I'm happy to help any way I can."

"Good," Tony said and then added, "The Back Alley Killer...that was some work. Sure glad to have you on my side."

Sarah thanked Tony and then hung up the phone. Then she began to wonder who might not be so glad that she was in town to help poor Bonnie Malloy.

Chapter Three

Getting Bonnie to agree to drive down to the local police station—which was nothing more than a squat, old brick building smaller than a diner—wasn't a simple task. After the phone call with its tragic news, Bonnie had transformed from an excitable, unpredictable host into a blubbering teenage girl who had lost the love of her life, a tormented widow, within a matter of seconds. Even though she had known him for only a month and not been married to José, her grief was as deep—and, Sarah thought privately, as loud—as if they had been lovers and partners for decades.

"Why?" Bonnie howled from the backseat of the rental SUV Sarah was driving. Sarah winced at the loud cry and swerved to avoid a snow-covered mailbox. "Why did José...poor, sweet, José...have to die? Oh José...my sweet darling...why?"

Amanda glanced over at Sarah and fought back a grin. The situation was far from funny, but Bonnie's melodramatic howls were amusing in their intensity and operatic noise. "How much farther, love?"

Sarah stopped at a snowy four-way stop sign, glanced around at the streets lined with homes straight out of an old fifties sitcom, and then checked the GPS attached to the dashboard. "Few more miles, I guess," she said and turned right on Dove Mill Road.

"Why!" Bonnie howled again and furiously dabbed at her tears with mittens that were thick enough to give a polar bear a toothache. "Why...oh, José, my sweet darling...why…come back to momma my sweet Señor...oh, come back to momma and let her wipe soy sauce off your chin..."

Amanda bit down on her lip so hard she almost brought blood. Sarah quickly tapped Amanda's arm and begged her friend to hold in her laughter with a desperate look. "Uh...Bonnie," Sarah quickly spoke, "you sure live in a pretty town."

"What do I care about that now that my sweet Señor has gone to his maker?" Bonnie howled through another fit of sobs. "Oh, how is my heart going to be able to handle this nightmare? How can I ever look at Chinese food the same way again?"

"With chopsticks," Amanda giggled under her breath. Sarah fought back a grin and then elbowed her arm again. "Sorry, love," Amanda whispered.

"Oh, my sweet José...the killer has struck at you in order to run me off my property...oh, my darling knight...so brave...so valiant..." Bonnie continued to howl.

Sarah gripped the steering wheel and struggled to focus. Certain questions began to arise on her mind. What was José Lopez doing in Bonnie's toy store? Was José the one who had been threatening Bonnie? Who had killed José? How did the killer get into the toy store? She didn't even know the basic facts, and Bonnie was in no state to answer her yet. Sarah's detective mind raced, wondering if Bonnie had employees, or security cameras. "I guess I'll find out soon enough," she whispered and didn't say another word until she reached the small downtown of Four Ridges. "Quaint," she told Amanda, driving down the main street past buildings and storefronts dating back to the fifties, like most of the houses they had passed.

Amanda studied snow-covered shops lit with glowing lights. A bakery with cakes in the window, a clothing boutique, a hardware store, a lawyer's shingle hanging on one corner. Further down she saw a restaurant and an antique shop that shared a storefront with a candy shop. The street, the stores, and shops blanketed by snow mingled together to create a lovely and very cozy small-town atmosphere. It was, Amanda reflected, a very American town; something she didn't see in larger cities she'd visited in the country. "Maybe we can have a go at that clothing boutique before we leave?" Amanda asked Sarah and pointed to a brick building glowing with warm lights and mannequins in the window showing off a fetching winter dress and soft sweaters.

"Maybe," Sarah said, checked the GPS, and slowed down under a blinking yellow light. "The police station should be..." Sarah looked to her left, turned onto a small side street, and then nodded. "There."

Amanda saw a little brick building sitting off by itself in a snowy lot. Two black and white old-fashioned police cars were parked in front of the building. "Wow. Welcome to Mayberry."

"Oh, José," Bonnie howled from the back seat. "My sweet Señor...come back to momma, my sweet little chili pepper."

Amanda let out a burst of laughter before she could stop herself. "Oh...so sorry..." she called out to Bonnie and cringed, waiting for the woman to explode. Instead, Bonnie continued to howl in misery.

Sarah wiped her forehead and quickly parked in the snowy police station lot. "Cousin Bonnie," she said in a serious voice, "Detective Massio needs to speak with you, okay? I understand you're upset, but you're going to need to pull yourself together."

"How can a widow answer questions at a time like this?" Bonnie asked as tears spilled from her wide, red-rimmed eyes. "My sweet José is dead...my sweet chili pepper...oh, come back to momma...don't leave her a widow..."

"Well, technically, love, you're not a widow," Amanda pointed out, trying to comfort her, and then immediately regretted her statement.

A dark cloud quickly filled Bonnie's eyes. She raised her mittens and struck the back of Amanda's seat. "Go back to England!" she screamed. "Can't you see that I'm drowning in agony? And you...you just...just..." The darkness faded from her furious eyes as she seemed to almost forget where she was, gazing about the car. "Oh dear...oh my...Amanda, sweetie...I didn't know what I was saying. I meant..."

"It's okay, love," Amanda promised in a quick voice and jumped out into a light falling snow before Bonnie could hit the back of her seat again.

Sarah sighed. "Come on, Cousin Bonnie," she said, climbed out into the snow, searched the white landscape, and shook her head. "Bonnie, I didn't see your toy store when we drove through town. Exactly where is it?"

Bonnie made her way out of the back seat, closed the back

door, and pointed north. "My toy store sits next to the town hall, a few streets over," she explained, wiped at her tears, and sighed. "I'll always see my sweet José walking through the front door of my toy store." She gazed in that direction.

A toy store next to a town hall seemed strange. "Bonnie, how long have you owned your toy store?" At least she was answering questions, Sarah realized.

"Why, twelve years," Bonnie exclaimed. She wiped her face again with her mittens, smearing tears and snot everywhere. "When I bought the building, there wasn't nothing around but empty lots." Bonnie trudged over to Sarah on sad legs. "I wanted my toy store to stand alone...to be different...special. That's why I chose the building I did. I was going to buy up the other empty lots and turn it into a park for the children, but then..." She made a sad face. "But oh, Sarah, I made my toy store very special...children love my toy store...everyone loves my toy store. But..."

"But what?" Sarah asked, spotting a vintage tan Oldsmobile approaching.

"We got a new mayor," Bonnie explained. "Mayor Heath Mooreland is his name."

Amanda eased over to Sarah and Bonnie. "Why would that affect your toy store? Is this Mayor Mooreland a sour bloke?" she asked Bonnie.

"A what?" Bonnie asked in a confused voice.

"A rat," Sarah said in a simple voice. "A bad person, Cousin Bonnie."

"Oh...well, yes, as a matter of fact he is." Bonnie nodded up and down, up and down, up and down. Poor Amanda had to look away. "Mayor Mooreland had the old town hall turned into a bookstore and bought up all the property around my store and had a new town hall built right next door to me...of all the nerve!" Bonnie kicked at the snow with her angry boots. With her bright red ski coat and blue ski pants, her muffler hat jammed down over her crazy-colored curls, she looked about as silly as a clown. "The new town hall doesn't even look like...well...like everything else in town. It doesn't look like the old town hall, I'll say that for sure."

"Oh?" Sarah asked, watching the Oldsmobile turning into the police station parking lot. She tried to steer Bonnie toward the door, not wanting to continue their conversation out in the open, but Bonnie was reluctant to move.

"Yes, it's all fancy...and it's two-story...our small town don't need a fancy two-story town hall," Bonnie said in a matter-of-fact voice. "Waste of money, if you ask me."

"Cousin Bonnie, when did Mayor Mooreland take office?" Bonnie asked in a quick voice.

"Last year," Bonnie explained. "I didn't vote for that...that...what did you call him?" she asked Amanda.

"Sour bloke?"

"I didn't vote for that sour bloke," Bonnie finished just as the Oldsmobile parked next to Sarah's SUV. Bonnie threw her eyes at the Oldsmobile and made a sour face. "Oh look. Another sour bloke has just arrived."

Sarah watched a man step out and walk towards them, his large belly causing him to waddle a little bit. He wore a grungy pair of tennis shoes and a faded brown hat that might have been a fedora a long time ago but was now all out of shape. "Detective Massio?"

"Detective Garland," Tony said, aiming for a cool tone even though his eyes belied his excitement at meeting Sarah.

"Actually, I'm married now," Sarah explained and held up her wedding finger. "My married name is Sarah Spencer."

"Who cares," Tony told Sarah, staring into the woman's beautiful face. "I'm standing before the woman who caught the Back Alley Killer."

"Uh...well, that was some time ago," Sarah explained. "The Back Alley Killer is—"

"Dead. I know," Tony blurted out. "I read all about how he found you in Alaska and tried to seek his revenge...real detective-novel stuff." Tony glanced at Amanda. Amanda was beautiful. "Who are you?" he asked with a crooked grin.

"I'm Amanda Hardcastle and I'm happily married," Amanda warned Tony, reading the man's eyes. "So don't make a pass at me, chubby, or I'll deck you square in the nose!"

"Hey, did I make a pass?" Tony asked and held up his hands. "Cool it." Amanda shook her right fist at Tony as one last warning. Tony quickly focused back on Sarah. "I was living in Los Angeles when you caught the Back Alley Killer. I don't suppose you remember me? I was a rookie at the time, just visiting for some training."

"I'm afraid not," Sarah confessed.

"I guess you wouldn't," Tony sighed. "I wasn't even a detective then," he explained and then looked at Bonnie. "Nice to see you, Bonnie."

Bonnie snapped her arms together across her chest. "I shouldn't even be here...my poor, sweet José is dead..."

"Yep," Tony nodded, "and you're my number one suspect."

"I thought she was just a person of interest, not a suspect," Sarah interjected.

"A suspect?" Bonnie screamed as a dark cloud rushed into

her eyes. "How dare you accuse me...I'll kill you!" she yelled and charged at Tony with her mittens held out in the snowy air.

"Hey...calm down...cool it!" Tony begged and dashed behind Sarah. Sarah barely had time to understand what was happening before Bonnie grabbed her right arm and sent her flying into Amanda. Amanda lost her balance, stumbled back against the SUV, and they both toppled down onto the snow-covered parking lot.

"I'll kill you!"

Sarah raised her head just in time to see Tony try to run a few steps in the icy parking lot before Bonnie tackled him down onto the ground like a linebacker, slapping at his head with her mittens. "Cousin Bonnie!" she screamed and climbed off Amanda.

Amanda struggled up onto one knee and watched Sarah charge at Bonnie. "Why me?" she whimpered and hurried to help Sarah save Tony from getting beaten senseless. "Bonnie...love...get off the poor bloke," she begged and grabbed one of Bonnie's arms. Bonnie reached up, grabbed Amanda, and slung her into Sarah. Sarah caught hold of Amanda but wasn't able to keep her balance. She tripped over her boots and went flying backwards again.

"Kill you...kill you!" Bonnie yelled and went back to beating Tony with her mittens.

"You okay, love?" Amanda asked Sarah and rubbed her back.

Sarah let out a moan, rubbed her own back, and nodded. "It's like trying to fight a raging bull."

"Get her off...get off me!" Tony begged, struggling to block his face from Bonnie's angry blows, her mittens sodden with snow. "I can't breathe...she's too heavy...get her off me!"

"Kill you!" Bonnie yelled, huffing and heaving with breath at her exertion. "Kill..." she started again, and then heaved a sigh. Just as quickly as Bonnie's fit of rage arrived, it left. The woman looked down at Tony for a second, glanced over at Sarah and Amanda, and then said, "Oh dear...oh my...this was a bad episode." Bonnie hurried to her feet, brushed snow off her legs, and rushed into the police station. "I'll be in the little girls' room freshening up," she called out. Her blushing cheeks were visible as she ran.

Sarah looked at Amanda, shrugged her shoulders, and then went to help Tony. "Are you okay?" she asked.

"She's insane...she should be locked inside a white padded room..." Tony began slapping snow off his trench coat. "You saw her...you saw how she attacked me. Is there any doubt that she killed José Lopez?"

"Actually, yes," Sarah confirmed. "Detective Massio, it's been my experience that jumping to conclusions is very unwise without evidence, and—"

"Jumping to conclusions?" Tony roared. "That woman almost killed me! I'm going to arrest her for assaulting an officer of the law...use of deadly weapons—"

"Deadly weapons?" Amanda asked.

"Her mittens," Tony declared. He stammered a little at the look of confusion on their faces. "They were...wet. Practically frozen with snow. She scratched me!" He cradled a tiny red scratch, not even bleeding, that had risen like a welt on one cheek. Sarah wasn't so sure he hadn't done that himself, judging from his unkempt nails and how he had been flailing around on the ground.

"Oh, good grief," Amanda rolled her eyes at Tony. "Did someone put a tablespoon of stupid in your oatmeal this morning?"

"Watch it," Tony warned Amanda. Amanda jutted out her jaw defiantly.

"Detective Massio, the point I'm trying to make is that a good cop investigates every possible lead, studies every piece of evidence, creates numerous theories, and chases down every last shadow before forming a conclusion," Sarah explained. "If you arrest her now for the murder, a lawyer will have her out in five minutes because you don't have enough probable cause. Besides, my cousin was receiving death threats—"

"Yeah, Bonnie showed me the letters," Tony confessed and looked around for his cigar. He spotted it lying in the snow, damp and broken in two. "See, that oversized freakshow even destroyed my cigar."

"You're not so fit yourself, Detective." Amanda nodded at Tony's large belly. "Been hitting the donut shop a little hard, haven't we?"

"Okay, that's it, you're under arrest for—"

"Oh, cram it in your ear," Amanda snapped at Tony. "You couldn't arrest a donut before it made its way to your mouth."

"Amanda...please," Sarah pleaded. She turned her attention to Tony. "A man is dead, Detective Massio. It's your duty to find out who killed him and why. And, if you would like, I will assist you. But not if you insist on turning this into a farce. We have to do it right."

Tony gave Amanda a sour eye and then shrugged his shoulders. "Fine...no need to get uppity about it. Anyway, with this being my first homicide...maybe it wouldn't be such a bad idea if you did help me. But," Tony added in a stern voice, "I'm telling you right here and now that Bonnie Malloy is the killer. You saw how she attacked me...you saw her have that little...fit of anger, or whatever it was. That counts for something."

"When it comes to murder," Sarah warned Tony, "don't stop looking in the first trash can you find." Sarah looked around at the snow and then focused her eyes on the police station. "Detective Massio," she said, "when it comes to murder, you must learn that the killer is always in charge. The killer is waiting for you to make a mistake." And with those words, Sarah walked into the police station. Amanda quickly stuck her tongue out at Tony and followed her best friend inside.

Chapter Four

Now that the questioning was officially underway, Sarah was dismayed to learn Bonnie wasn't interested in answering any of Tony's questions. "I need to check on my toy store," she protested in a childish voice and wiped at her nose with a blue handkerchief. "Yesterday I had a new shipment of vintage toys come in all the way from a dealer in Missouri. I haven't even unpacked the toys yet. Was there any damage in my store when you found my sweet José? Please, I need to go there."

Tony picked up his coffee mug and took a drink of hot chocolate. He didn't care too much for coffee. "Calm down, Bonnie," he griped, "we can't take you to an active crime scene. Besides, you should be glad I didn't arrest you for assaulting an officer of the law. I can still charge you for that, you know."

Bonnie shot Tony a sharp look. "You're just mad because I broke up with you all those years ago," she snapped.

Amanda, who was taking a sip of coffee out of a brown

paper cup, nearly spit coffee across Tony's cramped office. "You two were an item?" she asked.

"You bet," Bonnie claimed in a disgusted voice. "My psychiatrist said I was on the rebound. It was nothing."

Sarah watched Tony make a sour face at Bonnie. Boy, Bonnie and Tony were a pair. "Maybe we should go investigate the toy store and leave her here in custody?" she asked Tony in a quick voice, deliberately moving the current conversation to a new topic before Bonnie exploded into a fit of rage.

"Why?" Tony asked. "I already investigated it. The body was cold. It was taken to the morgue at the hospital. I called the state and arranged an official autopsy, reported the death to the right family members, had Mac take photos of the crime scene...dusted for prints...all by the book, nice and tidy," he finished in a proud voice.

Sarah nodded. Tony didn't seem like the smartest man, but at least he knew how to do his job; or at least he knew enough to follow standard investigative procedures, which were clearly laid out in the handbook sitting on the man's cluttered desk. "I still want to have a look around."

"Bonnie will have to come along," Tony said with an unhappy look. "We don't have anyone who can supervise her in custody. Like I said, we don't get murders here. It's kind of a one-man operation."

"No, you have to take me along because it's my toy store!" Bonnie yelled.

Sarah stood up and eased Bonnie over to a window fitted with a wooden blind. She opened it a little. "Never mind that...look at that snow, Cousin Bonnie."

Bonnie shot Tony a sharp eye and then looked at Sarah. "Oh, I'm acting silly, aren't I?"

"You're upset," Sarah replied and patted Bonnie gently on her arm. "However, we must all try and remain calm and reasonable in the face of tragedy and danger, okay?"

Bonnie smiled through her tear-streaked face. She sure loved her cousin. "You got it."

Sarah smiled back and then turned to face Tony's old wooden desk. His office was crowded with battered furniture, including a rusting metal filing cabinet and a wooden bookshelf full of comic books rather than law manuals. "Why me?" she thought miserably. "Why did I get stuck with a wannabe Dick Tracy and an insane cousin?"

"Look," Tony told Sarah, "we can't go over there, with her or without her. The mayor has made it clear—"

"The mayor?" Sarah asked in a quick voice.

Tony nodded. "Mayor Mooreland," he explained and continued. "Mayor Mooreland has ordered me to shut down the toy store and—"

Bonnie swung away from the window and aimed her red, blazing eyes at Tony. "What?" she yelled. "What did you say about my toy store?"

Tony quickly yanked out a Glock 19 that he wasn't very good at handling, aiming it shakily. "Now you stay back, Bonnie...don't make me shoot you," he warned in a shaky voice. "The mayor ordered me to close your toy store down. It's not my call...so you go put a knife in his back, not mine."

Sarah raised a firm hand at Bonnie. "Calm down, Bonnie," she ordered and then looked around the office as her mind made a few mental notes. "Tony," she finally spoke, "tell me about Mayor Mooreland. Who is he? Is he a native of Four Ridges? What are his political views?"

Bonnie huffed at Tony and went back to the window

mumbling under her breath. Amanda let out a sigh of relief, polished off her coffee, stood up, and pointed at the office door. "I need to use the ladies' room. Bonnie, love, do you need a break?"

"I guess it wouldn't hurt to freshen up," Bonnie complained and followed Amanda out of the stuffy office, sending a wave of relief crashing down into Sarah's heart.

"Don't ask me why I dated her," Tony ordered Sarah in a stern but embarrassed voice.

"I wasn't," Sarah assured the chubby detective. She plopped down in Amanda's chair and folded her arms over her coat. "Tony, tell me about Mayor Mooreland."

"I don't know that much about him," Tony confessed. He quickly finished off his hot chocolate and then pulled a Fifth Avenue candy bar out of the top righthand drawer of his desk. "Want one?"

"No, thanks," Sarah said and waited for Tony to continue.

Tony took a bite of his candy bar and then tossed a large thumb at the office window toward city hall. "I'm not a fan of politics. I see people eat others alive on social media sites over politics...it's enough to make a man wonder what has become of America." Tony shook his head. "When Mayor Mooreland won against the old mayor, Matthew Bellmore, I didn't think much of it. It's a small town. The mayor isn't that powerful. I mean, I didn't even vote, so what was it to me?"

"How long have you been living in Four Ridges?" Sarah asked.

"A while. Maybe five years."

Sarah nodded. "You're still new to this town and the people then."

Tony shrugged his shoulders. "I eat at the local diner a lot.

People know me and I know them. I mean, let's face it, Four Ridges isn't Los Angeles. It doesn't take long to get to know a few faces."

"Small towns can be deceptive," Sarah warned Tony. "You might be surprised at what you don't know. But listen, let's get back to Mayor Mooreland. Tell me, what do you know about him?"

Tony gave Sarah a curious eye. "Are you thinking the mayor is involved with the murder?" he asked and then let out a goofy laugh that bounced off the office walls. "Detective Garland—"

"Spencer."

Tony laughed again and shook his head. "Maybe you've been retired too long, reading too many novels," he said. "Mayor Mooreland is the last person who would be involved in a murder. The man is seventy-five years old and should be in a nursing home, for crying out loud."

Sarah looked down at her hands and thought for a minute. "Is Mayor Mooreland married?" she asked, ignoring Tony's statement.

"I guess," Tony nodded. "I heard there was a Mrs. Mooreland, but I never met the woman."

"Does Mayor Mooreland have any family living in Four Ridges?"

Tony shrugged his shoulder. "Beats me."

Sarah raised her eyes. "Find out," she ordered Tony in a tough cop voice. "Stop giving me half answers, is that clear? We're investigating a murder case, and I don't have time to deal with your lame-brain attitude. Either you're going to give me your best or take a hike."

Tony paled. "Hey...I'm a good cop...I investigated that

crime scene. I'll show you the case file. But what does Mooreland have to do with anything? Besides, I'm in charge, not you."

"I can make a few phone calls and kick you out of the driver's seat," Sarah warned, hoping to bluff Tony. "You know I have contacts in Los Angeles and New York. Michigan isn't new to me, either. Don't make me pick up the phone."

Tony dropped his candy bar and raised his wide hands up into the air. "Okay, okay...calm down...sheesh," he begged. "I'll do some digging into Mayor Mooreland's family tree," he promised Sarah. "Okay?"

"Better," Sarah said, keeping her voice tough. "Now, here's how we're going to play this, Tony," she continued. "Someone killed José Lopez and is trying to pin the murder on Bonnie Malloy. Why? That's what we have to find out."

"Oh, come on...Bonnie—"

"Isn't the killer," Sarah snapped at Tony in a voice that made Tony sit up straight. "You said the body of José Lopez was cold, right?"

"Yeah...kinda cold."

"And the blood on his back and on the floor was dry, right?" Sarah pressed.

"How did you know? Yeah it was...dry," Tony nodded, struggling to catch up to Sarah's thinking. "I guess the body seemed to have been dead for a while."

"Then do some detective work in your mind," Sarah demanded. "Where was Bonnie Malloy last night, when José was killed? She told me she was home all night working on her computer, ordering new toys for her store."

"That's what she said, sure," Tony reluctantly nodded.

"So let's see if her alibi is solid." Sarah waited until Tony nodded again, following her line of thought. "Bonnie said she used the landline in her house to call a dealer in Georgia. Check with the phone company and see if her story matches up," Sarah said.

"Bonnie could have slipped out of her house during the middle of the night," Tony insisted.

"Then check with the security company that Bonnie uses and see if the alarm pad was deactivated anytime during the night. Check with her neighbors and see if they saw her leave, heard a car running, or a taxi drive by. Pound the pavement and do some detective work, Tony. If you think Bonnie is the killer, then start knocking her statements into the trash and prove she's a liar. Until then, by her own statements, the woman claims she's innocent. So she's innocent until proven guilty." Sarah drew in a breath. It shook her a little to order Tony to investigate her own cousin like this, but it was necessary. "What do you have on José Lopez?" she asked, moving on to the next important part of the investigation.

Tony straightened in his chair, trying to meet her eyes. He was desperate to not look like a rookie cop. "José Lopez," he said and quickly dug through the mess on his desk and pulled out a brown folder. "Okay, here we are." Sarah watched Tony scan through the folder's contents. "José Lopez...age fifty-four, divorced...one daughter. He moved to Four Ridges last year...works for Solid Grounds Development, a land and real estate company. He lives at 231 Milton Drive, Apartment 4C. He drives a new KIA..." Tony looked over the folder with proud eyes. "I had Mac run José for me after he finished with the prints. We're trying our best here, you know."

Bonnie stood in the doorway, Amanda hovering behind her. Seeing the two detectives still at work, the pair wandered off to find a coffee pot.

Sarah, however, paid no attention to Bonnie and Amanda, and didn't hear a word Tony said as he continued to review the file. "Solid Grounds," she whispered in a deep, thoughtful voice and then closed her eyes and began walking up and down the cozy main street in her mind. "Solid Grounds Development...it all makes sense," she whispered again.

"What?" Tony asked.

Sarah opened her eyes. "One second," she told Tony, pulled a cell phone out from her coat pocket, and called Pete.

Pete was in his office chewing on a cigar and going over a case file when the phone on his desk rang. "Yeah, yeah," he fussed and yanked up the phone. "Mrs. Peals, I'm reviewing —" he began to bark.

"I'm not Mrs. Peals, Pete," Sarah said and waited for Pete to begin fussing at her.

"Oh, it's you, kiddo," Pete complained in a gruff voice. "Did you call to say you're sorry for nearly getting me killed in London?"

"Oh, Pete," Sarah begged, "I had to use you as bait, it was the only way to catch our killer."

Pete rolled his eyes. "Bait," he huffed. "I taught you everything you know, and you used me as bait."

"We caught a deadly killer because you did teach me everything I know," Sarah told Pete, trying to soothe his wounded pride.

"Don't sweet talk me," Pete fussed. "Just tell me what you want."

"Solid Grounds Development Company, Pete."

"Is that who I think it is?" Tony gushed. "Is that Pete—"

Sarah nodded and waved at Tony to hush. "I'm in Michigan, Pete. Seems like someone is trying to pin a murder on my Cousin Bonnie. We already have a stiff."

"Bonnie Malloy?" Pete asked in a shocked voice.

"Yes."

"Isn't she your cousin who's a little…uh…special?" Pete asked, wishing he hadn't decided to wear suspenders to work. He yanked on the back of his pants to work a wedgie free.

"Yes, Pete, but she's innocent."

Pete walked behind his desk and sat down. "Listen, kiddo, I'm up to my ears with Mrs. Peals. Her husband is missing and she's chewing my ear off day and night for answers."

"Is he really missing?" Sarah asked.

"No, of course not. I tracked him down," Pete said in a disgusted voice. "The guy is living with his brother in Malibu. Why? Because he's hiding from the police. Why? Because he faked his death. Why? Because he stole a whole lot of money from the bank he was working for." Pete spit his cigar out. "My only problem is deciding what to do with him."

"Oh?" Sarah asked.

"Mrs. Peals doesn't know, but I know she's hired herself a gunman to make sure her husband really ends up sleeping with the fishes. It's a mess…but don't worry, kiddo, I'll find the time to run this land development company and see what I can dig up. Call me tonight."

"Thanks Pete, you're the best," Sarah beamed.

Something in Sarah's voice made Pete roll his eyes. "Your compliment tells me you want another favor."

"Mayor Heath Mooreland, the current mayor of Four Ridges, Michigan. See what you can come up with, Pete," Sarah asked in a sweet, innocent voice.

"This coming from my partner who used me as bait in an old opera house...and I hate opera!" Pete growled at Sarah. "I should dump you into the ocean instead of helping you."

"I know...I know..." Sarah winced.

Pete rolled his eyes. "Call me tonight, kiddo."

"I will," Sarah promised and then remembered something. "Oh, how did you appointment go with the cardiologist?"

A happy smile replaced Pete's gruff demeanor. "I had a heart catheterization done, kiddo. Doc said my heart was clear as a bell and pumping like a man in his forties. My stomach doctor ran a tube down my throat and told me that I looked good down there, too."

"That's the best news ever, Pete," Sarah said in a relieved, happy voice.

"Yeah, yeah, don't go getting mushy on me. I've got work to do. Call me tonight."

Sarah smiled and put her cell phone away. "Okay, Tony," she said and stood up, "I got my guy working on some background. Let's go get Amanda and Bonnie and drive to the toy store. I'll make sure she doesn't muck up your crime scene, but we gotta get going—"

"You were talking to...Pete...the legend," Tony interrupted in a shocked mumble, staring at her. "Pete...you were...talking to Pete. You really do have contacts."

Sarah rolled her eyes, walked over to Tony, grabbed his arm, and pulled the large man to his feet. "Toy store...murder...remember?" she asked, rolled her eyes, and pushed Tony out of the stuffy office.

At that same moment, at City Hall, Mayor Mooreland walked into his fancy, spacious office and made a private call.

"It's me," he said in a cold tone. "Tell Mr. Capps that it won't be long before we begin tearing down this town and building a new one...and no one is going to stand in our way...no one."

Chapter Five

Bonnie Malloy's store, Vintage Toys, sat in a quaint, cozy brick building that had been painted to look like a peppermint candy cane. The two display windows in the front of the building glowed with warm light, displaying nostalgic toys hinting at better days gone by. Sarah spotted old G.I. Joe figures surrounding a sweet Care Bear town with protective love, a Cabbage Patch village that had a classic train set circling it carrying My Little Pony figures as passengers, and other toys that opened up locked doors in her memory. The falling snow also lent a helping hand in transforming a simple painted brick building into a cheerful vision, like a dream filled with gumdrops and presents, echoing with the laughter of innocent children.

However, the new town hall right next door to Bonnie's store told another story. Its austere, modern landscape and fancy finishes cast an ugly eye at the toy store's humble facade, the new building looming tall and looking down its nose at Bonnie's careful cultivation of innocence and childhood joy.

"Very cozy," Sarah told Amanda as she waited for Bonnie to duck under the yellow police tape and unlock the antique wooden door decorated with a sign reading "Let It Snow," words held by a sweet snowman surrounded by falling candy.

Amanda tossed a worried thumb at the new town hall. "That building looks like a city office," she whispered in a disgusted voice. "Every office you see today looks the same...cold, unfriendly, and very ugly."

Sarah looked over to the town hall and studied the building. At that moment, a deep gray drape covering a second-floor window flew open. Sarah squinted her eyes and stared up at the window through the falling snow. A hideous-looking old man appeared at the window. The old man cast a deadly eye down at the scene taking place at the toy store. He watched Bonnie unlock the front door and then slapped the gray drape closed. "Mayor Mooreland," Sarah whispered.

"Come on inside," Bonnie called out. "Tony, you bozos didn't even reset the alarm system," she griped, fussing with the alarm box by the door.

Sarah looked at Tony. Tony winced, shrugged his shoulders, and then hurried into the toy store. "Please let this go well," she whispered to herself and took another look around before leaving the cold. "Snowy woods...street that is basically bare of houses and businesses...not a bad spot for a greedy land developer to sink his teeth into."

Amanda hugged her shoulders. "Love, can we talk inside? I'm starting to turn into an iceberg."

Sarah nodded and quickly walked Amanda into the toy store. "Oh my," she gasped as her eyes took in the interior.

Amanda froze. "Oh my..." she whispered in shock. "It's...like walking into a dream..."

Sarah slowly closed the front door and then let her eyes wander around like an excited child. She glanced down and spotted a red and white peppermint floor with a cozy green and white choo-choo train large enough for small children to ride in sitting silent in a sleepy corner; small passenger carts shaped like teddy bears were attached to the choo-choo train. Gingerbread walls decorated with button candies, gum drops, and chocolates waited amid snowy blankets of fluff that surrounded the life-size doll houses filled with dolls and chairs and tables and beds and lamps...oh, so wonderful, Sarah thought as her eyes drifted off to a play area marked off with red and white wood that held enormous, plush teddy bears. Next she saw a treehouse that had been built and stationed in the far corner of the store; a snowy tree had been built to hold a cozy gingerbread treehouse filled with G.I. Joe figures, tanks, play guns, plastic Army men, every toy a little boy needed to play war with. Next Sarah let her eyes investigate rows and rows of quaint wooden shelves that held every vintage toy a person could imagine. Lastly, she gushed to see a small library area that resembled a toy workshop, complete with children's construction books and little tools. "Build Your Imagination" a cozy sign read in bold, colorful rainbow letters. "Bonnie...this is amazing."

Bonnie walked over to a wooden counter that had been carved to look like a choo-choo train hauling tons of toys and checked an old-fashioned cash register. The cash register dinged as she opened the drawer. "Hey, this is empty. I left twenty dollars in here!" she yelled and then spun around to face Tony. Tony grimaced and then, to Sarah and Amanda's disappointment, pulled a twenty-dollar bill out of his coat pocket. "Thief!"

"Evidence," Tony insisted. "I just haven't got around to putting the money into an evidence bag and filing it yet. Honest, Bonnie."

Bonnie snatched the twenty out of Tony's hand and then prepared to slap him when all of a sudden a happy, tingly feeling washed over her. "Oh, how I do love my toy store," she almost chirped, forgetting about Tony as she nearly danced over to Sarah and Amanda. "Years of work, but I created a special place for children to...be children."

"Yes, it's very lovely," Sarah replied, shocked that her cousin—a woman who could have escaped from a mental hospital—had created such a beautiful and warm toy store. Perhaps, Sarah thought, somewhere deep inside of Bonnie, an innocent childlike heart helped her understand children. That innocent heart had helped her to create and operate a very special toy store. After all, wasn't Bonnie—minus her frightening "episodes"—sometimes more like a child herself? A child trapped in a woman's body, trapped inside a mind that struggled with the realities of life while fighting to stay ten years old? "Very lovely, Cousin Bonnie. I'm impressed."

"Yes, love," Amanda gushed as her eyes soaked in the warm dream before her, "your toy store...my...it's like...walking into a new world...a better world."

Bonnie grabbed Sarah's and Amanda's hands and squeezed them so tight that both women nearly cried out in pain. "Oh, it is, isn't it?" she giggled. "I used all the money my parents left me...well, almost all of it. I had to buy the house I live in...but I still drive momma's old car," Bonnie giggled again. "Sometimes I get stuck in third gear, but don't tell nobody."

Tony looked at Bonnie like she was insane. "This is why

we broke up," he said and rolled his eyes. "These crazy mood swings of hers drove me batty. One minute she was happy and then angry for no reason at all."

Sarah quickly shook her head at Tony and told him to shut up with her eyes. It was too late. A dark cloud exploded over Bonnie's head. Bonnie spun around and pointed a dangerous finger at Tony. "You watch your mouth before I pulverize you!" she yelled.

Tony quickly hurried behind the front counter. "Now you calm down, you hear me?" he yelled back. "If you step one foot toward me, I'll pull out my gun and shoot you!"

"You just try it!" Bonnie screamed and then...the black cloud vanished, and joy returned to her eyes. "Oh, let me show you girls around," she beamed at Sarah and Amanda, grabbed their hands, and began an excited tour through the toy store. Sarah and Amanda looked at each other, shrugged their shoulders, and simply enjoyed the tour as Tony leaned on the front counter and grumbled unhappily to himself. "This is the Atari section," Bonnie explained in an excited voice.

Sarah looked at wooden shelves that had been specifically designed to house Atari items. Everything was custom-made. There were even vintage Atari signs attached to the wooden shelves, all in pristine condition. "Just look at all those old games," she said, studying neatly organized rows of Atari games as if they were priceless gold.

"And over here," Bonnie yanked Sarah and Amanda over to another wooden shelf and happily pointed to a very rare set of GoBots and then focused on a set of shelves holding every Looney Tunes character in existence. "All of my toys are in perfect condition," she said in a proud voice.

Amanda checked the price on a Daffy Duck figurine and whistled. "I can see why."

"Oh, money doesn't matter when it comes to toys," Bonnie laughed merrily. "Besides, a gal has to know what to charge in order to keep her head above water, right?"

"Uh...right," Amanda smiled, carefully placing the figurine back in its spot.

Sarah spotted a wooden door that led into the back storeroom. "Cousin Bonnie, can you take me into the back room?"

"Oh sure, not a problem," Bonnie beamed, apparently having completely forgotten about José Lopez. That was the way her mind worked. The poor woman could only focus on one topic at a time, unable to multi-task different thoughts and emotions at once. "Follow me."

Sarah looked at Amanda. "Go keep an eye on Tony, June Bug," she whispered. "I don't want him to disturb me, okay?"

"Keep an eye on the fat guy. Got it, boss." Amanda grinned, tipped a wink at Sarah, and hurried away.

Sarah laughed to herself. "Okay, Cousin Bonnie, let's go."

Bonnie smiled and walked Sarah into a warm brick room that, to Sarah's surprise, was plain and practical. No special designs, no gingerbread trim, no candy canes...just brick walls, wooden shelves and a hardwood floor. "Can I be alone?" she asked Bonnie, spotting a white chalk outline on the floor. Tony had chalked the position of José Lopez's dead body.

"Sure, sure," Bonnie beamed. "I'll go show that sweet friend of yours around some more. Maybe I'll let her ride my train. Oh, so exciting!" Bonnie clapped her hands and dashed out of the storage room like a girl rushing out to her prom.

Sarah whistled to herself and then walked over to the

white chalk outline, knelt down, and began to study the floor. She spotted spots of dried blood leading away from the chalk outline. "Blood trail..." Sarah bit down on her lip and began a slow duck walk as her eyes followed the blood, which took her straight to the back door. "José Lopez wasn't killed in this toy store. His body was brought inside." Sarah stood up, unlocked the back door, and looked out into a small back parking lot big enough for a box truck to maneuver, but nothing larger. Beyond the parking lot stood miles and miles of snowy woods. "I wonder..." Sarah stepped out into the snow, walked to the east side of the building, and stopped. "Easy access," she said, spotting the rear of the town hall building. Nothing separated the toy store and the town hall except a long flowerbed that was now bare and covered with snow. "My bet is on José Lopez being killed in the town hall and the body was dragged into the toy store," Sarah muttered to herself.

Sarah studied the back of the town hall with careful eyes, memorizing the layout, and then returned to the storage room. She closed and locked the door and went back to the chalk outline. "Okay...let's see..." Sarah whispered and began studying the position José Lopez's body was found in. "Arms stretched out...legs apart..."

A scream from Tony interrupted Sarah's study. "What now?" she grumbled, stood up, and ran into the toy store. She spotted Bonnie taking a swing at Tony's head. Tony ducked just in the nick of time and barged behind one of the life-size dollhouses. "Bonnie...stop it!" she demanded.

"He called me fat!" Bonnie screamed, face red. "I'll kill him!"

Sarah looked around and then spotted Amanda, who rose

up from behind the front counter and waved a shaky hand into the air. "Are you okay?" Sarah begged.

"I'm alive," Amanda replied in pain and rubbed her back. "She just knocked me over a bit, that's all."

Bonnie began to charge toward the dollhouse. Tony let out a cry and began fumbling with his gun in its holster. "Stay back...I'll shoot you...shoot you where you stand," he threatened Bonnie as his trembling hands fought to free his weapon from an expensive holster that Sarah immediately noticed wasn't a proper fit for his Glock 19. Just like Tony himself, that holster was all style and no substance. "Get back, you overstuffed nightmare, before I make you regret it! You cannot assault an officer of the law!"

Bonnie ignored Tony's threat and continued her charge. On her way over to the dollhouse, she grabbed an enormous plastic candy cane out of a wooden box. "I'll bash your head in!"

"Cousin Bonnie!" Sarah yelled in a tone that caused Bonnie to stop in her tracks. "Put down that candy cane right now! Do you hear me? Right now! Unless you want to be handcuffed. You can't keep doing this! And you," Sarah yelled at Tony, "if you're going to pull a gun on an innocent woman, try to do it without shaking like a schoolboy, okay?"

Bonnie stared at Sarah and then, to Sarah's relief, put the candy cane back in its box. "He called me fat," she mumbled under her breath like a pouting child.

"Watch your mouth," Sarah warned Tony. "There's no call for insults. We're at a crime scene. Act professional."

Tony nodded like a scolded child sent to the corner. "Yes, ma'am."

Sarah shook her head at Tony and then walked over to

Bonnie. "Bonnie, we're all a little out of sorts, I think. Maybe you can make us all some coffee?"

Bonnie's eyes slowly lifted up off the floor. "I suppose I could," she pouted. "I suppose coffee would be nice. It is a cold morning."

"That's my girl," Sarah smiled and gently patted Bonnie on her hand. "In the meantime, I have to talk with Tony in the storage room, okay?"

"I suppose that would be fine," Bonnie sighed and then let her shoulders droop. "I'm not...I'm big boned, Cousin Sarah. Always was."

"I know, honey," Sarah promised and then dragged Tony into the storage room. "Okay. Where is the murder weapon?" she demanded.

"The murder weapon?" Tony asked. "Oh, the knife...it's in the trunk of my car."

"Go get it."

"But...the knife has blood all over it," Tony objected. "I...Dr. Green...dislodged the knife from José Lopez's back for me. I'm a little squeamish, you know."

"Fine, give me the keys to your car. I'll get the knife myself," Sarah sighed, feeling tired and a little hungry. It was going to be a long day.

"Why do you need to see the knife?" Tony asked. He tossed a thumb down at the chalk outline. "José Lopez was stabbed in the back, right here in this room. That's pretty open and shut."

"Is it?" Sarah asked, pointing to the blood trail on the floor leading to the back door. "I suppose after he was stabbed, he got back up and made a nice little trail to the back door?"

Tony looked embarrassed after squinting down at the

drops. "I didn't see that was blood," he claimed and then sighed with his hands on his hips, drooping a little like Bonnie had earlier, Sarah noticed. "I guess I'm just a stupid cop."

"You're not stupid," Sarah told Tony. "Just...inexperienced. Now—" Sarah was interrupted by Tony's cell phone. Mayor Mooreland was calling.

Chapter Six

"What are you doing bringing all those people to the toy store?" Mayor Mooreland demanded in a voice that could have thrown a thousand sharp knives at Tony. He stormed across a dark burgundy rug and snatched back the drape covering his office window. "I ordered you to close the toy store, Detective Massio. Did you not understand me?"

Tony bristled at Mayor Mooreland's rude attitude but didn't have the guts to say so. "Mayor, a man has been killed and it's my job to investigate fully. We must bring justice to—"

"Don't give me that line!" Mayor Mooreland snapped. "I gave you a direct order, Detective!"

Tony felt sweat beading on his forehead. He looked at Sarah nervously, unsure who would chew him out worse; the big-city detective or his stone-cold boss. "Mayor, my job—"

"I know what your job is!" Mayor Mooreland narrowed his eyes and continued to study the toy store as intent as a snake stalking a nest of rats. "Who are those women I saw you with?"

Tony hesitated and then told Mayor Mooreland about Sarah and Amanda. "Mayor, Detective Garland caught the Back Alley Killer. She's famous. If anyone can help me solve this murder, it will be her," he finished in a quick voice.

Sarah folded her arms and observed Tony's facial expressions as he talked to Mayor Mooreland. The man was nervous, angry, and uncertain all at the same time. However, this was more than the man's usual bluster and bumble. Whoever Mayor Mooreland was, Tony Massio didn't care for the guy, and, from the tinny shouting she could hear over the phone, it appeared the feeling was mutual. "You say this detective is Ms. Malloy's cousin?" Mayor Mooreland said.

"Yes," Tony answered. "And the other woman with her is Amanda Hardcastle, a woman from London. Her best friend."

Mayor Mooreland kept his eyes on the snowy toy store. "I see," he said as his mind began to turn over the implications. Having a strange detective in town would surely cause problems; two strangers would surely only make it worse. Controlling an idiot like Tony Massio was very simple—not so simple, however, to control a seasoned and famous murder detective. Mayor Mooreland had read about the Back Alley Killer and even saw Sarah conduct a television interview about the famous killer she had caught. And, to make matters worse, when the killer had tried to strike at Sarah in Alaska, the media attention began all over again, throwing an otherwise fading name back into the spotlight. "Why did Detective Garland want to visit the toy store?" he asked Tony, forcing a calmness to his voice.

"Well, her married name is Spencer," Tony quickly added, "I guess we should use her married name, Mayor."

Mayor Mooreland squeezed the cell phone he was holding. "Why did Detective...Spencer...want to visit the toy store?" he asked, seething with impatience.

Tony looked at Sarah. Sarah saw his mind struggling to find answers. She shook her head and told Tony to hand her the phone. Tony happily obliged. "Mayor Mooreland, this is Detective Sarah Spencer. How can I help you?"

"You can begin by telling me why you're trespassing at a closed crime scene," Mayor Mooreland answered in a sour voice. "I ordered that store closed."

"Mayor," Sarah explained, forcing her tough police voice back into action, "I traveled to Four Ridges to assist my cousin, who has been receiving death threats in the mail. I arrive here only to find out that your police department has done nothing to track down the culprit. Now, the man my cousin was dating is dead and my cousin is being suspected of murder. You'll forgive me if I'm not the most trusting of the Four Ridges police squad." Sarah knelt down and studied the chalk outline on the floor again. "I'm going to have some of my friends in law enforcement call your governor and ask him to give me the green light to work on this case. I'm also going to call the governor's office in Alaska and let them know what's going on and then contact some friends in the press. I want to bring as much attention to this case as possible. An innocent woman, threatened with death and ignored by the police, is being framed for murder. I will not let that happen."

The color drained from Mayor Mooreland's sour face. "Is that really necessary?" he asked.

"It will be if you try and interfere," Sarah explained. "I've already contacted a friend of mine in Los Angeles and have him working on a few leads for me. My husband, who is also a cop, knows of my location and he'll be assisting me very soon as well." Sarah studied the drops of dry blood on the ground as she built a protective wall around herself and Amanda. If Mayor Mooreland attempted to kill them, he would be wise to realize how many outside sources were aware of the situation. Sarah's hunch was that this whole crime stank of a cover-up, with Mayor Mooreland at the center of the web of lies. Killing one man may have been simple...but Sarah was going to make sure he knew killing anyone else would be vastly more complicated.

"Detective Spencer, I only have the best interests of Four Ridges in mind," Mayor Mooreland explained, assuming a colder, more practical tone. "It's my duty as mayor to put the town and its citizens in a position of safety and security." He walked away from the window and returned to his dark mahogany desk, idly toying with an ivory box full of expensive cigars. "I also have my own safety to consider. That's why I ordered the toy store closed," he lied. "Whoever killed Mr. Lopez might have done so as a warning to me."

Sarah saw right through Mayor Mooreland's slimy lies. However, she knew enough to know that a corrupt politician never walked into a situation blindly. Surely Mayor Mooreland had a few aces hidden up his sleeve to protect himself in the crooked card game he was playing. "Of course," Sarah replied in an equally cold voice. "Mayor Mooreland, as of right now I don't have any direct leads—"

"But," Tony began to object. Sarah shot him a stern eye. Tony winced and stepped over to the back door and pulled a cheap cigar out of his coat pocket. "I thought she said the blood trail was important," he mumbled under his breath.

Sarah rolled her eyes. "I've examined the toy store, Mayor," she continued. "From what I've seen, Mr. Lopez was killed in the storage room."

"Yes, I'm aware of that, Detective."

"Good," Sarah said and watched Tony fidget with the cheap cigar, "because as of now, that's all I've got...I'm going to check a few leads—"

"Such as?" Mayor Mooreland demanded. He sat down in a brown leather chair, then opened the ivory cigar box and fetched out a cigar. He felt far more secure knowing that this meddlesome detective seemed more gullible than she first appeared.

"I'll inform you of my progress when it's time," Sarah explained. "Right now, I need to do some more investigating and see what I can dig up. However, as it stands, I'm afraid my cousin might have to defend her innocence in front of a jury." Sarah closed her eyes and prepared to bluff Mayor Mooreland. "Whoever killed Mr. Lopez, in my opinion, was a professional. The storage room is cleaner than a whistle. The leads I do have are minuscule at best...it's going to be very difficult to help my cousin, I'm afraid."

Mayor Mooreland enjoyed this turn of events. Was the woman actually asking him for a favor? He decided to play the woman for the fool she was. "Detective Spencer, you may contact anyone you deem necessary. Rest assured, my office will not interfere with your current endeavor to assist Ms. Malloy."

"That's good to hear," Sarah replied, pretending to sound

relieved, "because I didn't want to bother with a bunch of political sharks...no offense."

"None taken." Mayor Mooreland retrieved a white ivory lighter out of his pocket and placed it down on the desk. "I'm certain Detective Massio will also appreciate your assistance," he continued. "Detective Massio is...relatively new to his position. I worry he is not experienced enough to accept the challenges of this case. With your help, I'm sure he'll do just fine." His voice dripped with smooth amusement.

In other words, Sarah thought, Mayor Mooreland was saying Tony was too stupid to tie his own shoes and that's exactly the way he wanted to keep it. "I'm happy to help Detective Massio," Sarah said, continuing the ruse. "As a matter of fact, he's already done an excellent job ensuring that the proper protocols were followed."

"Of course," Mayor Mooreland smirked. "In the meantime, Detective Spencer, please keep me updated on all your progress. As a matter of fact, I would like to have daily reports delivered to my office. After all, this is the first murder that has ever taken place in Four Ridges, and the people of this community are looking to my office for answers."

Sarah could have vomited. "I'll do my best," she told Mayor Mooreland and ended the call before Mayor Mooreland could say another word. "Here's your phone."

Tony walked back to Sarah and took it from her. "I thought you said Bonnie Malloy was innocent?" he asked without taking the cheap cigar from his mouth.

"Tony," Sarah explained, "you have to know sometimes a cop has to bluff."

"Bluff...the mayor?" Tony asked and then rolled his eyes. "Are you still thinking that old man has something to do with the killing? I've already told you that he's one step away from needing a nursing home."

"He may be elderly, but his mind is sharp as a tack," Sarah pointed out, trying not to give in to irritation. She reminded herself how patient Pete had been with her at the beginning. "Mayor Mooreland doesn't have crippled hands or a crippled mouth. He can easily hire a person to do his dirty work."

Tony paused in shock. "But this is Four Ridges...we're just a little tiny town in the middle of nowhere, America. Surely hired killers only happen in the big cities."

Sarah tapped the chalk outline with her boot. "Murder can happen anywhere, Tony," she explained. "José Lopez worked for a land development company. Bonnie Malloy was receiving threatening letters that told her to vacate this building or die. Mayor Mooreland had a new town hall built. Any of this ringing a bell?"

Tony slowly removed the cheap cigar from his mouth and tried to think. It was easy when there was a book to follow, with steps printed out in black and white right before your eyes. But to step outside the book and look at the messy reality of crime...now that was a challenge. Tony had never been good at critical thinking skills. Life was black and white and the stuff in the gray zone, well, stayed in the gray zone. "I still think Bonnie Malloy killed José Lopez. She could've been... jealous, I don't know. Maybe she killed him outside and dragged his body in here?"

Sarah shook her head. "Then it's up to you to prove that," she told Tony.

"I intend to," Tony promised, even though his voice wasn't so confident. "I'm going to call the security company and check the alarm pad logs. The alarm pad had to be disarmed, right?"

"Seems that way."

"Well, I'll start there," Tony said and strutted out of the storage room like a proud rooster.

Sarah rolled her eyes. "Why me?" she asked and then walked to the back door and checked the deadbolt. As far as she could see, the lock had not been tampered with. Of course, Sarah knew the lock had not been tampered with from the first moment she entered the storage room, but she needed time to think, and looking around for small clues couldn't hurt. "Okay, Mayor Mooreland, the chessboard has been set...let's see who's going to win," she whispered. Turning away from the deadbolt lock, her eyes caught on a shelf of baby toys secure in their packaging. Little soft shapes and charming colors beckoned to Sarah. Without realizing it, she reached down and touched her belly. "Someday..." She ached, thinking of how much she wished she were home with Conrad, planning a nursery and filling it with such things. But before Sarah could finish her thought, she saw the chalk outline just nearby, and that same hideous snowman in a leather jacket appeared in her mind, a vision of everything dark in her life. *Always murder, Sarah...death and murder...I never go away. You'll never have a sweet baby in a life like this... you're trapped forever...this life almost got you killed at the hot springs, remember? You got real sick...someday that sickness will come for you out of the darkness...someday you're going to escape this dark life, but only because you'll die...*

Sarah squeezed her eyes closed against the terrifying vision. "Go away...go away..."

"Love?"

Sarah opened her eyes and spun around. She saw Amanda standing in the doorway. "Is everything alright?"

Amanda lifted up a coffee cup shaped like a gingerbread house. "I thought you might like some coffee," she answered and walked over to Sarah with worried eyes. "Are you alright?" she asked and looked Sarah deep in her eyes. "Was it...the snowman?"

Sarah slowly took the gingerbread coffee cup from Amanda. "It's always the snowman, June Bug," she explained in a miserable voice. "The snowman never leaves me alone. It's in my dreams...my thoughts...my heart...hunting me every day." Sarah took a sip of coffee. The coffee wasn't half bad. "I wish we were home in our coffee shop...or home shopping at O'Mally's...or…home getting a nursery ready."

"Oh love." Amanda carefully hugged her best friend. "I wish we were home, too. I wish we were preparing to spend the entire day at O'Mally's shopping until we popped."

"Dropped," Sarah corrected Amanda with a gentle smile.

"Oh...yes...dropped," Amanda smiled back and patted Sarah's hand. "I would suggest we leave this town, but I'm afraid your cousin would kill that cop and really end up in hot water."

"That's true," Sarah agreed with a sad little laugh. "June Bug, I'm afraid we're dealing with some very dangerous people who want to turn the town of Four Ridges into something horrible." Sarah showed Amanda the blood trail on the floor. "José Lopez's body was dragged into this storage room," she explained. "We have a very difficult case ahead of us, June Bug," she warned and took a sip of coffee. "We're not dealing with a small-town thug. Mayor Mooreland didn't sound like a man who was new to this kind of thing."

Amanda looked down at the chalk outline and felt a cold shiver grab her spine. "It never becomes real until you see it...in person," she told Sarah. "Maybe we—"

"I'll kill you!" Bonnie's voice thundered into the storage room.

"Oh no, not again," Amanda moaned.

"Come on," Sarah begged and ran out of the storage room with Amanda, leaving behind a single contact lens on the floor, hidden in the dusty corner—an eye contact that belonged to the man who killed José Lopez.

"Bonnie...put down that candy cane!" Sarah's voice echoed out into the snow, landing on the wings of icy winds that howled around Mayor Mooreland's office window. Yes, the chessboard was set—another snowy chessboard filled with killers.

Chapter Seven

Bonnie slapped Tony so hard with the candy cane she was holding that the man's head nearly went flying off his shoulders. "Bonnie!" Sarah cried.

Tony wobbled on his feet, looked at Sarah with disoriented eyes, and then hit the floor and went off into a deep sleep. "He called me a killer!" Bonnie told Sarah in a furious voice and then...the dark cloud covering her eyes vanished and a look of puzzlement came over her face. "Oh my...oh dear..." she gasped, looked down at Tony's unconscious body, and made a guilty face.

Sarah quickly took the stick away from Bonnie. "I should have cuffed you myself, innocent or not. If I wasn't so certain who was really behind the murder of José Lopez, I would swear you killed him," she fussed, unable to control her anger.

"Kill my José?" Bonnie asked, then remembered. "Oh...my sweet Señor José!" Bonnie howled. "Oh, my sweet chili pepper...come back to momma...don't leave her a widow!"

Sarah watched tears begin falling from Bonnie's large eyes. "Oh, good grief," she whispered, placed the candy cane stick back in its box, and looked at Amanda. Amanda began to speak, but Bonnie grabbed her before she could say a word.

"Oh, José!" Bonnie howled. "Oh...come back to momma...come back..."

Amanda began waving her arms in the air as if she were a bird preparing to take off. "Bonnie...love...can't breathe…air, love...need air."

"Oh, José!" Bonnie wailed, ignoring Amanda's plea.

Sarah rolled her eyes, ran over to Bonnie, and pried Amanda free. "Bonnie...honey...get a grip," she begged.

Amanda backed away from Bonnie, gasped for air, and then rubbed her sore rib. "Uh...we should get out of here. I'm feeling a bit hollow. Lunch anyone?" she asked.

Bonnie's tears abruptly stopped flowing. "Lunch?" she asked and then happily smiled. "Yes, lunch. The diner is serving turkey and stuffing today." Bonnie clapped her hands. "I love turkey and stuffing, don't you?"

"I'm not so certain Tony will be hungry," Sarah told Bonnie and tossed a thumb down at the unconscious man. Bonnie looked at Tony and made another guilty face. "Honey, you have to control your temper," Sarah begged, knelt down, and examined Tony. "He has a bad bump on the side of his head...might be a concussion."

"He...called me a killer," Bonnie pleaded with Sarah. "I...everything went red for a minute. I'm sorry."

Sarah glanced up at Bonnie—glanced up into the face of a child trapped in the body of a woman—and sighed. How was she going to handle someone whose childlike wonder seemed so at odds with her childlike temper? She dressed like a clown dancing around a silly circus tent, but she was capable of real violence. She switched moods faster than a melting snowflake in the hot sun. "Bonnie, you assaulted a cop...Tony now has every right to arrest you...and he probably will. But let me do it...I need to arrest you before he wakes up angry."

"I'm sorry," Bonnie began to cry. "Cousin Sarah...I didn't mean to hit Tony...he called me a killer...I saw red. Please don't arrest me."

"Love...you are an adult woman. You can't let your temper control you and whack someone upside the head with a candy cane," Amanda told Bonnie, deliberately keeping her distance from the woman. Her rib was too sore to take another hug. "An adult woman like you is capable of acting with grace and charm, not brute force."

"I guess you're right, Amanda," Bonnie sighed and kicked at the floor like a pouting child kicking a tin can. "Momma always said I had a bad temper. I don't mean to cause any harm."

"Honey," Sarah said in a voice that was filled with desperation, anger, fatigue, and sheer exasperation, "why do you get so angry?"

"Because people make fun of me," Bonnie explained, keeping her eyes low. In her mind she saw a room filled with children. All the children were mocking her and calling her names. "People always made fun of me, Cousin Sarah. Why? Because I was different." Bonnie slowly raised her eyes. As she did, a tear—an honest, authentic tear filled with pain—fell from her eye. "I didn't ask to be born into a body that looks like a brick wall. I didn't ask to look like a linebacker who plays for a professional football team. I didn't...ask to be made fun of by all the pretty girls."

Amanda felt her heart break for Bonnie. She dared to

move closer and wipe the woman's tear away. "Oh love, you're beautiful in your own way."

"No, I'm not," Bonnie objected, focusing with great effort. "I have eyes, Amanda. I look into the mirror every morning and see this…ugly face. But what can a woman do except accept her fate and try and be happy?" Bonnie caught sight of the choo-choo train and immediately switched tracks. "Besides," she said in a cheerful voice, "that's why I have my toy store. My toy store makes me very happy. If only people understood that happiness is more important than outer beauty…"

Sarah watched Bonnie trail off, gazing around at her massive toy store, and looked at Amanda. "Will you drive Bonnie to the local diner? I'm going to take Tony to the hospital and have his head checked." She decided an arrest could wait, if Bonnie was willing to go along nicely.

"Sure, love," Amanda told Sarah. "Bonnie, let's go get some food, because this woman is starving."

"You bet," Bonnie clapped her hands. "We'll have a girl's day out…just you and me." Bonnie swung her eyes at Sarah. "The code to the alarm pad is 1929. Don't forget to set the alarm." And with those words, Bonnie grabbed Amanda's hand and pulled her out into the falling snow. Amanda gave Sarah a desperate look and vanished out into the white wonderland outside.

"Poor baby," Sarah sighed, feeling sorry for Amanda, and then knelt to wake Tony up. "Come on, wake up…wake up, Tony…wake up," she said, gently slapping Tony's cheeks. A few minutes later, Tony's eyes fluttered and slowly opened. Sarah let out a sigh of relief. "Wake up," she told Tony. "You're okay."

Tony looked up into a blurry but beautiful face and smiled. "Hey, you're beautiful..."

Sarah rolled her eyes. "Come on, get up, Tony," she ordered in a stern voice. She grasped Tony's left arm and helped the man slowly lean up. "You took a nasty hit to the noggin."

Tony felt pain explode through his head like a tidal wave crashing down. "You're telling me," he moaned, rubbing his skull carefully. "What happened?"

"Uh...Bonnie...took a swing at you with one of those," Sarah explained and pointed to the box of candy cane sticks. "She made contact with your head."

Tony rubbed the side of his head, felt the tender bump that had formed, and moaned. "I'm going to arrest her...no, I'm going to hang her."

Sarah didn't argue. "How about we overlook this one offense...at least until we get you to the hospital?" she asked in a hopeful voice and carefully helped Tony stand up. The man was awkward and inflexible, which made the task of helping him stand up quite a workout. "You really need to lay off the donuts, Tony. I'm not joking."

"You're insulting a wounded cop?" Tony asked in a sour voice.

"If you got into a foot chase with a deadly criminal, how would you do?" Sarah asked and wiped sweat off her forehead. "You know what, forget it," she told Tony, feeling hunger and fatigue wearing down her emotions. "Let's get you to the hospital and have you checked over. You might have a concussion."

"No way...no hospital for me," Tony objected.

"You need to see a doctor. Bonnie really got you good, Tony," Sarah explained. "You were out for quite a while."

Tony touched the side of his head again, winced in pain, and looked down at the floor. "I don't like doctors, okay? I'll be fine. Just...drive me back to my apartment. I'll rest for the rest of the day and be back at my desk tomorrow morning."

The idea of having Tony out of her hair appealed to Sarah. If he had symptoms, she would drive him to the hospital the next morning if need be. "If you insist," she said and quickly set the alarm, and then helped Tony outside into the snow. "Let's move," she said, noticing the snow falling heavier than before.

Tony let Sarah help him into the passenger seat of the Oldsmobile and then closed his eyes. "Stupid woman," he mumbled under his breath, "hit me in the head with a candy cane...gotta arrest her."

Sarah tossed a careful eye at the town hall, jumped into the driver's seat of the Oldsmobile, and drove away from the toy store confident that Mayor Mooreland would leave the store untouched. "How are you feeling?"

"Like a deranged lunatic hit me in the head with a candy cane," Tony fussed.

Sarah focused on the snowy road. "Where do you live?" Tony lifted his right hand and pointed north. "I need a street name."

"Pine Lake Lane," Tony mumbled. "Keep driving. I'll tell you how to get to my apartment."

"I'm going to keep your car for the rest of the day and pick you up tomorrow morning," Sarah told Tony. Tony waved a hand of approval into the air. Sarah nodded, drove Tony to his apartment, dropped the man off into the snow, then hurried back to town.

Poor Tony watched Sarah drive away, wandered into his messy one-bedroom apartment, and crashed down on a couch, moving aside a few candy bar wrappers and potato chip bags. When a man was depressed, he ate. Why was Tony Massio depressed? Because he was lonely...and broken inside of his heart. All Tony desired was to be loved by a good woman, to get married, have a family, and live out the rest of his life like a sitcom dad. Instead, he had nearly lost his badge in Los Angeles, had to beg a friend to help him secure the job in Four Ridges, and now he was living alone in a crappy apartment, working a lousy job, eating himself senseless. "At least I have my donuts," Tony mumbled and then passed out with his face stuck to a potato chip bag.

Sarah, unaware of Tony's emotional hardships, drove back to town, spotted the red rental SUV parked in front of the local diner, drove past, and made her way to the police station. "Need to think," Sarah said, swinging the Oldsmobile into the parking lot in front of the police station. She parked, jumped out into the snow, retrieved the murder weapon from the truck, and made her way back to Tony's office. To her relief and dismay, the police station was completely empty, not a soul in sight. "Nice," Sarah groused, walked into Tony's messy office, shut the door, sat down behind the cluttered desk, and examined the knife that had killed José Lopez. "Plain kitchen knife..." Sarah whispered, resting her hand on her chin. "Blood trail on the floor..." Sarah kept her eyes on the kitchen knife in its large plastic evidence bag. "Blood trail on the floor...plain kitchen knife..." she whispered over and over again and then tapped her chin. "José Lopez wasn't killed with this knife.

Whoever killed him stabbed this knife into his back after he was dead and then positioned his body on the floor."

Sarah picked up the bag holding the knife, stuffed it in the top desk drawer, and then called Conrad. "Hey, honey, it's me," she said, dreading the phone call.

"Uh oh," Conrad said, reading Sarah's voice, "what's wrong?"

Sarah pictured Conrad sitting at the kitchen table in their cabin sipping on a hot cup of coffee and reading the daily newspaper with Mittens asleep in her doggy bed. "How is your ankle?"

"Sarah, what's wrong?" Conrad demanded. He put weight down on the wooden cane in his left hand and waited for Sarah to explain. "Honey?"

Sarah bit down on her lip. "Well, Conrad...it seems like my cousin is in...trouble."

Conrad closed his eyes and began tapping his fist against his forehead. "I had a feeling...I had a feeling..." he groaned.

"Please don't be upset," Sarah begged. "A man has been murdered and Bonnie is in the spotlight."

"Of course, she is," Conrad groaned again. "Sarah, honey, wherever you go there's always a murder..." Conrad shook his head, looked down at the old gray robe he was wearing, and then glanced over at Mittens. Mittens was hard and fast asleep. "I'll find someone to take care of Mittens and—"

"No, stay home," Sarah pleaded. "Conrad, I can handle this case."

"Sarah, you nearly got yourself, and Pete, killed in London. On top of that you didn't even inform me you were chasing a killer until the mess was all cleaned up," Conrad fussed.

"I'm telling you now...dear...honey...sweetheart," Sarah told Conrad, desperately trying to make her voice sound as sweet and loving as possible. She felt like Lucy trying to pull a fast one on Ricky. "Besides, I already know who the killer is and the motive for the murder. All I have to do is set a trap and catch myself a rat."

"Sure...sure," Conrad complained, "it's that simple, right? Murder is always a walk in the park."

"You know better than that, honey," Sarah replied in a distraught voice. "Look, Conrad, this isn't my fault. Bonnie is in serious trouble, and there's no way the local detective...a real winner, let me tell you...can help her. The local detective is convinced that Bonnie is the killer." Sarah rubbed her eyes. "Honey, I have to help my cousin. The woman is...helpless in so many ways...and out there, too...way, way out there."

"We're supposed to be trying to have a baby," Conrad reminded Sarah. "I took you to London hoping the trip would help us. Instead, you got caught up in a murder case. And now, once again...murder." Conrad closed his eyes. "Sarah—"

"I know," Sarah told Conrad and touched her belly with a soft hand. "You have every right to be upset."

"And you have every right to be a cop," Conrad replied. He drew in a deep breath and steadied his emotions. "We're both cops, Sarah. We can't walk away from our duties...no matter how much we want to."

"Sometimes I regret the day I chose to become a cop," Sarah confessed. She looked around Tony's cluttered office and sighed. "Don't forget to walk Mittens, okay?"

"Don't forget to shoot first and ask questions later, okay?"

Sarah felt a relieved smile touch her lips. "You know me too well, honey."

"I mean it, Sarah."

"I promise," Sarah told Conrad. "I'll shoot first and ask questions later."

"Aim low and—"

"I know how to manage my firearm, honey," Sarah assured Conrad.

"Call me every hour."

"I will." Sarah closed her eyes, saw a dead man lying in the storage room of Bonnie's toy store, and then saw a hideous snowman appear beside the dead man. "Conrad?"

"Yes?"

"I can't let him win," Sarah whispered, told Conrad she loved him, and then ended the call with fear in her eyes. "I can't let him win..." Sarah wasn't afraid of Mayor Mooreland; she was afraid of the darkness haunting her nightmares.

Chapter Eight

Bonnie waved an excited hand at Sarah. "Over here!" she yelled.

Sarah watched a chubby waitress in her early sixties roll her eyes at Bonnie as she walked a cup of coffee over to a yellow and white booth where an old man read a newspaper. "Over there," she told Sarah and then added in a sarcastic voice, "Try not to get lost."

"I'm sure I won't," Sarah replied in a cold tone and walked her eyes around the warm diner she had stepped into. The diner reminded her of the old place she used to frequent quite often while living in Los Angeles: linoleum floors (only the tiles under her boots were yellow and white instead of black and white), walls covered with movie memorabilia from the golden age of the silver screen, rows of booths and a juke box that appeared to be from...oh, Sarah guessed, the early sixties. A song from the jukebox was asking the age-old question, "Why must I be a teenager in love?"

"Over here!" Bonnie waved at Sarah again.

Amanda grinned, took a bite of a delicious double-stack

cheeseburger dripping with extra cheese, and waited for Sarah to join them. "How is Mr. Unconscious?" she asked as Sarah slid down next to her.

"Awake. Sorta. I took Tony back to his apartment," Sarah explained, removed her coat, and shoved it down onto her lap. "He refused to go to the hospital. There wasn't really much I could do." Sarah lowered her eyes and saw a stack of tater tots on a dark brown plate. Her mouth began to water. "I'm hungry," she admitted.

"Of course, you are," Bonnie told Sarah in a happy voice. "Oh, it's just us girls having lunch together! Isn't this exciting?"

"It sure is, love," Amanda smiled and nudged Sarah with her elbow. "This is my third plate of food. You've been absent for a while. What gives?"

"I drove back to the police station after I took Tony home," Sarah explained. "I needed time to think."

"And?" Amanda gently pressed.

Sarah looked across the table and studied Bonnie's eyes. "Bonnie, does anyone know the code to your security system?" she asked.

"Of course not," Bonnie replied and then smiled. "Cousin Sarah, I'm an independent woman who owns and operates a toy store. I know I'm not the smartest woman in the world, golly no, but I'm not stupid...although some people seem to think so."

Sarah quickly folded her hands together. "Honey, you're not stupid...so please don't get angry at me for asking this next question."

"Why, of course not. Ask away." Bonnie leaned forward

and waited anxiously for Sarah to ask the question, nearly spilling a tall, frosty vanilla milkshake in the process.

"Did you give José the code to your security system?"

Amanda watched Bonnie's face change from expectant to confused and embarrassed within a mere second. "I...uh...well..." Bonnie attempted to speak and then began stumbling all over herself. "Cousin Sarah, I...José, you see, asked me to take him on a private tour of my toy store...it was real late...I kinda...well, José served me some wine you see..."

Sarah offered Bonnie a tender nod. "It's okay, honey, I get the picture."

"Oh, I'm such a silly...dum-dum," Bonnie moaned. "My sweet Señor...oh my sweet José...do you think he betrayed me?" Tears began falling from Bonnie's eyes and dripping down onto a bright green and red sweater covered with silver winter bells. "I was wondering how someone got into my storage room..."

"Really?" Sarah asked in a curious voice.

Bonnie wiped at her tears. "I'm not stupid...oh, José...come back to momma...don't leave her a widow...she's too young."

Amanda tucked her head down and fought back a grin as the waitress approached their booth. "What's eating you now, Bonnie?" she asked in a sour tone. "Or are you practicing your tears for the judge?"

"You shut up, Florence," Bonnie snapped. "I'll slap you out into a snowbank if you don't!"

Florence held up her hands. "Oh please, don't kill me like you killed José Lopez," she begged in a sarcastic voice and then focused on Sarah. "What'll it be?"

Sarah spotted a sweet-looking waitress in her mid-forties

wiping down the front counter. The woman tossed an apologetic shrug at Sarah and then sighed. "Ma'am," Sarah called out to the other waitress, "will you come and take my order?"

"Have it your way," Florence told Sarah, rolled her eyes, and walked away.

Noel Shifton, who had only been working at the diner for a year, quickly patted her short brown hair smooth, brushed a few crumbs off her yellow waitress uniform, and hurried over to Sarah. "Hi, my name is Noel. Can I start you off with a coffee?"

Nathan Branch, the old man reading the newspaper—the long-suffering owner of the diner—smiled to hear Noel's cheery tone, then threw a warning eye at Florence. Florence rolled her eyes, threw down an order pad, grabbed a brown coat off the wooden coat rack beside the front door, and walked out into the snow, quitting without notice. "Mr. Branch?" Noel asked in a worried voice.

"You can handle your shift without that sour woman," Mr. Branch assured Noel, rattling his newspaper as he turned to the business section. "Mae and Paula will be here before the dinner crowd arrives." Mr. Branch then added, "You're now the new manager, Noel. Go see my wife in the back office when you finish with that order and tell her I said so. I suspect my wife will be very pleased at my decision."

"Manager?" Noel gasped.

Sarah smiled. "Congratulations."

"Oh...yes, thank you," Noel blushed. "Uh...may I get you some coffee?"

"Black coffee, a cheeseburger plate...extra well done, no onions or mayonnaise...tater tots and a slice of apple pie for dessert, please," Sarah placed her order. "Uh, can you make that two cheeseburgers? I skipped breakfast this morning and I'm really hungry."

"On the house," Mr. Branch called out over his newspaper. "We treat guests with respect in this town, especially if one of those guests is a celebrity."

"Celebrity?" Noel asked Mr. Branch.

Mr. Branch lowered his newspaper and nodded at Sarah. "That woman caught the Back Alley Killer. That deranged rat was terrorizing Los Angeles and nearly all of America, for that matter." Mr. Branch lifted his newspaper. "The same killer went after the woman you're looking at for a second time, but she put a rose on his coffin."

"Actually…my friend here killed the Back Alley Killer," Sarah explained in a quick voice. "The truth is, he would have killed me if Amanda hadn't acted first. She's the real hero."

"Oh," Amanda blushed, "Love, I'm not a hero. I was just cold, cranky, and a little quick with the trigger."

Mr. Branch lowered his newspaper and studied Amanda. "Make sure you wrap up a to-go plate for that woman. And don't forget the extra cheese on her cheeseburgers."

Noel looked down at Sarah and Amanda with shock. "I read about the Back Alley Killer, but why are you here?" She then tossed a careful eye at Bonnie. "Oh, I'm sorry…there's been a murder in town so…of course…"

"People believe Bonnie Malloy is the killer, right?" Sarah asked Noel.

Noel reluctantly nodded. "Mac came back for lunch," she explained. "He had his usual, but while he was here—"

"While he was here, he ran his big mouth," Mr. Branch fussed from behind his newspaper. "By the time he was finished, Mac Nelson had the entire lunch crowd believing Bonnie Malloy killed José Lopez."

Bonnie's eyes turned dark. "I'll deck Mac Nelson so hard—"

Sarah held up a quick hand, looking her cousin in the eyes for a moment to remind her of their discussion. "You don't seem the type to follow along blindly with a story like that," she told Mr. Branch. "Why?"

Mr. Branch lowered his newspaper. "Because I'm seventy-seven years old, that's why. I've been around the block a time or two. My old eyes know how to spot a rotten fish and a good apple. Bonnie Malloy is a good apple. A little odd, but a good apple, nonetheless. Besides, my grandchildren love her toy store. Takes a special kind of person to make a toy store like that."

"Oh yes," Noel beamed, "my kids love your toy store, Ms. Malloy. My husband, although he will never admit it, loves to visit your toy store and peruse the old Nintendo games."

The dark cloud snapped out of Bonnie's eyes and a ray of sunlight appeared. "I've seen you in my toy store before. You were always a very nice lady and you always treat me nice when I visit the diner," she smiled at Noel.

"Well, my ex-co-worker might not think so, but I believe in manners. Besides, Jesus tells us to love each other, Ms. Malloy," Noel smiled. "I teach my children the same truth."

Bonnie smiled from ear to ear. "Amen," she told Noel and then added, "You bring your children to my toy store when I open back up, and your husband, too. Tell them they can pick out any toy they want...on the house. And that includes you, too."

"Oh, my," Noel gasped, "Ms. Malloy, they'll all simply have a fit. Thank you so much."

Mr. Branch smiled from behind his newspaper. The rare moments when people showed kindness and love toward one another were precious. "Noel, you better go tell Jason to get busy on the new order before that woman starves."

"Oh...of course," Noel laughed, smiled at Sarah, and hurried away.

"Now that is a sweet woman," Amanda beamed. "I could just squeeze her to pieces and take her home with me."

"Me, too," Sarah agreed. She looked at Mr. Branch and decided to simply rest her mind and fill her hungry tummy before exploring any more dark alleys. "So," she told Bonnie, "for the rest of the day I thought it would be wise if you stayed inside your house with Amanda. I figured you two could bake up a storm—a girl's baking day. Does that sound okay?" Sarah was slowly, and carefully, learning how to play Bonnie's emotional strings.

Bonnie nearly exploded with joy. "Oh, yes," she nearly yelled and grabbed Amanda's tender hand. "You and me can bake muffins and cookies and brownies and—"

"Okay, okay, love," Amanda laughed, "we'll bake up a snowstorm." Amanda gently pulled her hand away from Bonnie. "But first I think I better use the loo. I've had four Dr. Peppers and now it's time to, uh, water the roses."

Sarah quickly let Amanda out of the booth. Amanda hurried away toward the restrooms, rubbing her hand where Bonnie had squeezed it. "She's so sweet," Bonnie giggled. "I like people who come from the land of chocolate."

Sarah sat back down. "Bonnie, you know Amanda is from London and...oh, never mind," she smiled.

Bonnie scooped up her milkshake and sipped from the straw. "I'm very regretful for needing so much of your help," she said as her mind quickly switched gears. "I know my behavior hasn't been ideal, and I'm sorry. My psychiatrist tells me that I suffer from...well, she says I keep my emotions all bottled up instead of confronting people when they upset me." Bonnie looked down at her milkshake. "Dr. Milsap said because I took that route for so many years now...well, you saw how hard I hit Tony...even though he deserved it. Anyway, I don't mean to keep having these outbursts the way I do, honest I don't. I can't control myself when...well, when that dark cloud covers my mind...at least that's what Dr. Milsap calls it. There's a real fancy medical term for it but I can't pronounce the word. I guess I'm not smart enough."

"Honey, you're a very smart woman...brilliant, as a matter of fact," Sarah promised. "I do wish you hadn't knocked Tony unconscious. But at least you didn't kill him," Sarah added in a positive voice.

"I didn't kill poor José, either," Bonnie pleaded. Her mind began to dwell again on the sadness of her lost love, but she somehow managed to stay focused on the topic at hand. "The person who sent me all those mean letters killed José. I just know it."

"Yes," Sarah agreed, knowing Mr. Branch was listening to every word. "Honey, I have a terrible feeling Mayor Mooreland is involved, too," she explained in a careful voice. So much for relaxing and not exploring dark alleys. "I have a feeling Mayor Mooreland is connected to the Solid Grounds land development company." Sarah paused, glanced at Mr. Branch, saw the old man slowly lower his newspaper just enough to slip his eyes over the top, and then continued. "Did José ever talk about his work?"

"No," Bonnie honestly answered. "But I already told you that."

"Yes, I suppose you did." Sarah leaned back and folded her arms. "Cousin Bonnie, before I left Tony's apartment, I made him give me the key to Jose's apartment. I'm going to investigate the apartment after I eat. I may or may not find anything." Sarah studied Bonnie. "Have you ever been to José's apartment?"

Bonnie felt her cheeks turn red. "Oh, just once. José cooked me dinner...tacos. Oh, the tacos were so good...a bit too salty...but good."

Sarah nodded. "What did the inside of the apartment look like?" she asked, spotted Noel walking a cup of coffee toward the booth, and smiled. "Looks good. Thank you."

Noel gently set the cup of coffee down. "Your order will be out shortly," she promised. "Is there anything I can get you while you wait?"

"The coffee will be fine, thank you," Sarah promised. Noel smiled and wandered away.

Bonnie picked up her milkshake and frowned. "Cousin Sarah, José was my sweet señor, but he had awful taste. His apartment...well, it was so...bland. As a matter of fact, his apartment looked as if no one even lived in it."

"Oh?" Sarah asked, picked up her coffee, and took a sip. "Not bad."

Bonnie lowered her milkshake. "Maybe that's just the way a man who isn't married lives?" she asked. "I didn't want to jump to conclusions. Golly, no. Momma taught me that when you're a guest in someone's home, you act respectful. It was just that...well, the tacos were good...bit too salty for my taste...but..."

"But what, honey?" Sarah gently pressed at the mind of a woman struggling to speak words that seemed to be causing her guilt.

"The dinner plates," Bonnie confessed. "The dinner plates were brand new, right out of the box," Bonnie admitted and then looked at Sarah with confused eyes. "Did my sweet señor not want me eating off his plates? Oh, I know that's a horrible thought, but...well." Bonnie sighed.

"Cousin Bonnie, did you have any wine during dinner?" Sarah asked.

Bonnie's cheeks turned red. "I'm afraid I did. That was the night José asked me to take him on a tour of my toy store."

"When was this?" Sarah asked.

Bonnie looked up at Sarah and saw a brilliant cop hard at work. It was sure nice to have family; or so Bonnie hoped— whoever killed her sweet señor might force Bonnie to end up one cousin short.

Chapter Nine

Bonnie convinced Sarah and Amanda to have one cup of coffee before leaving to investigate José's apartment. Sarah, feeling stuffed and ready for a nap after three cheeseburgers and two plates of tater tots, caved in and decided that one cup of coffee couldn't hurt. She followed Amanda back to Bonnie's house, parked in a driveway that had become covered with snow again, and hurried into a warm kitchen...and ran into a storm. "I'll get the coffee going in a split second and—" Bonnie began to speak as Sarah and Amanda followed her into the kitchen. Her words were cut short when a man wearing a gray hood appeared before her holding a gun.

"Inside...now!" the man hissed and aimed his gun right at Sarah. "That means you, cop!"

Sarah reached behind her back, grabbed Amanda's gloved hand, and carefully entered the kitchen. "Who are you?" Sarah asked just to buy a little time.

"Close the door!" the man ordered Amanda. Amanda drew

in a worried breath and slowly closed the back door. "Over there."

Sarah watched the man wave his gun toward the kitchen table. "Do as he says, Cousin Bonnie," she warned without telling anyone she detected nervousness in the intruder's voice. Whoever the man was behind the mask, he wasn't a professional killer.

Bonnie shot a sour look at the man but didn't say a word. She walked over to the kitchen table and plopped down like an angry little girl. "Gonna get snow all over my kitchen floor. I just mopped the kitchen floor last night, too," she grumbled.

Sarah motioned for Amanda to sit down next to Bonnie and then took a seat herself, without disclosing her gun that was hidden in an ankle holster attached to her right ankle. "What do you want?"

The man holding the gun hurried over to the kitchen door and locked it. "This is a warning," he hissed, desperately trying to sound tough. "Leave town or die."

Sarah took a few seconds to study the man. The man was fat—really fat. The black sweatshirt he wore over a pair of black jogging pants made him look like an Orca. Sarah could smell his filthy sweat. "Is that all?" she asked in a calm voice. She waited to see what he would do. Whoever the fat man was, Sarah doubted he had the guts to kill three innocent women. No. The fat man was only a messenger—someone who had obviously watched too many mafia movies and decided playing a role might be fun. The man fidgeted as he watched them through his mask. "Is that all?" she said.

And then, without understanding why, she saw the image of the old black man she had become close friends with in Oregon appear in her mind. She saw the old man sitting on his front porch watching the sun set, staring out over his beautiful pumpkin field, humming a sweet hymn. *Stay calm, girl,* she heard the old man tell her in an easy voice as he worked on a corn cob pipe filled with cherry tobacco. *Stay calm and let time take its course. No sense trying to rush the Good Lord's ways. Be who you're meant to be in the moment and let tomorrow worry about itself, you hear?* Sarah heard the old man's sweet voice as if he were sitting next to her. She turned her head and, to her shock, saw the old man appear right before her eyes. *You're a cop, girl. Stop trying to be what you aren't, you hear me?"*

Sarah felt a soft breeze whisper away from a field of bright pumpkins and touch her tender face. "I want to have a baby," she nearly cried inside, silently. "What am I doing here?" The old man reached out a wrinkled hand, took Sarah's hand, and smiled. *Stop trying to rush the Good Lord's plan, girl,"* he said in a soothing voice. *What's meant to be will be...in time. Now you stop trying to be what you ain't, you hear me? That ugly snowman that's after you ain't going to stop chasing you. You can't just change your life.* Sarah made a pained face. "How do I kill it?" she begged the old man. The old man let go of Sarah's hand and touched her heart. *You can't stop your own nature, girl. If you ever stop being a cop, that snowman will kill you. Now I know you want a baby more than anything, but it ain't time to have a baby. There's a little more work to do, you hear?* And with those words the old man vanished before Sarah's eyes. Bonnie's kitchen around her appeared dull and confusing by contrast. "Is that the message?" she heard herself say without being aware she was talking.

"Listen, cop," the fat man snarled, his anxiety seeming to fuel his tongue, "my boss doesn't want to kill you, but he will if you don't get out of town with your friend there." The fat man aimed his gun at Amanda. "My job is to make sure you leave town."

"Oh?" Sarah asked, feeling her mind returning back to normal a little.

"I'm going to follow you to the county line," the fat man explained. "If you're smart, you'll keep driving. If you're stupid, if you turn around...I'll put a bullet in you and your friend...and then the only place you'll be going is six feet under the earth. Got it?"

"What if I refuse?" Sarah asked, feeling a strange sensation wash through her heart. She locked eyes with the fat man. "What if...if..." Sarah allowed her head to begin tilting from one side to the other. "Uh…oh my...I feel...faint. Amanda...I think one of my sugar attacks may be coming on…"

"Sugar attacks?" Bonnie asked in a confused voice. "Cousin Sarah, are you a diabetic?"

Sarah raised her right hand into the air and began feeling her face. It was time to pull one of the oldest tricks in the book. "I don't feel right...I hope I don't…faint," she said in a weak voice and then simply dropped out of her chair and struck the kitchen floor.

"Sarah!" Amanda cried out, playing along. She dropped down onto her knees and felt Sarah's head. "I need sugar, Bonnie...hurry."

"Hey, what is this?" the fat man demanded. "What's wrong with her?"

"My friend is having a diabetic attack," Amanda yelled. "I need sugar..."

Bonnie scrambled to her feet, believing Sarah was having an authentic attack, and ran to the refrigerator. She brushed past the fat man and knocked him to the side. The fat man quickly spun around and aimed his gun at Bonnie. "Get back to the table!" he ordered.

Bonnie ignored the order, yanked open the refrigerator, and pulled out a coconut cake. "You shut up!" she yelled at the fat man. "My cousin is a sick woman."

The fat man watched Bonnie slam the cake down onto the kitchen counter and then go for a plate. "Get back to the table," he yelled again and then made the horrible mistake of turning his back to Sarah. "Get back to the table now," he ordered, grabbed Bonnie's arm, and tried to yank her away from the kitchen counter.

"You let go of me!" Bonnie screamed and swung a wild right fist into the air.

The fat man let go of Bonnie's arm, stumbled a few feet back, and aimed his gun into the air. "Don't make me shoot you!"

"If you want to live, drop your weapon now!" Sarah's angry voice ripped through the kitchen air with force and authority.

"Huh?" the fat man asked. He spun around and saw Sarah on one knee aiming a deadly gun straight at his chest.

"Drop your gun!" Sarah yelled.

"You better do it, fat boy," Amanda said and tossed a thumb at Sarah. "My friend isn't in the mood to be nice to the likes of you."

"Hey...wait..." the fat man began to plead, feeling his courage drain out onto the kitchen floor in a gooey mess. "Hey...I was just...doing my job, you know...no hard feelings..."

"Drop your gun!" Sarah yelled, popped up to her feet, and narrowed her eyes. "Now!"

The fat man raised his shaky gun hand out and released his gun. The gun hit the kitchen floor, an ugly sound of metal against tile. "Okay...okay..."

"Take off your mask," Sarah ordered.

The fat man hesitated and then slowly pulled off his mask.

"Mac?" Bonnie gasped. "Mac Newman? But you're a...a cop," she stammered.

Sarah studied the man's chubby face. "A local cop turned bad," she said, sickened.

Mac Newman held his hands out to Sarah. "Look...we can make a deal, okay? I mean...it's all about money, right?"

"No," Sarah informed the crooked cop. "Sit down!"

"Okay...okay..." Mac hurried over to the kitchen table and sat down.

"June Bug, get his gun," Sarah told Amanda. Amanda quickly scooped up Mac's gun.

"So...you're not sick?" Bonnie asked Sarah.

"No, honey, I'm not sick," Sarah promised her worried cousin. "At least not physically."

"Huh?" Bonnie asked, confused.

"Put the cake away, love," Amanda smiled at Bonnie. "We'll explain later."

"Okay, if you say so," Bonnie replied, shrugged her shoulders, and put the coconut cake away. "Should I call the cops?"

"I am the cops, stupid," Mac barked before he could catch his tongue.

"Don't you ever call me stupid!" Bonnie picked up a plate and hurled it across the kitchen. Mac saw the plate flying at his head and then...he saw blackness, as the plate smacked him right above his eyes and sent his head flying backwards on his shoulders. "Oh dear...oh my..." Bonnie gasped.

"Bonnie...honey..." Sarah moaned as she watched Mac crumple down onto the kitchen floor. Bonnie made another unconvincing guilty expression and hurried to put the coconut cake back into the refrigerator. "Oh honey..." Sarah mumbled and then checked on Mac. The fat man was out cold. She swept aside the shards of the plate. "He'll live," she sighed and asked Amanda to retrieve her purse. "There's a pair of handcuffs in my purse, June Bug."

Amanda gathered Sarah's purse, fished out the handcuffs, and hurried over to the kitchen table. "Why did you have a pair of handcuffs in your purse, love?" she asked.

Sarah took the handcuffs from Amanda and quickly secured Mac's hands behind his back. "Old habits die hard, June Bug," she explained. "I guess a cop never leaves home without a gun and a good old pair of handcuffs."

Amanda studied Sarah's eyes and saw a woman who was both scared and angry. "What now, love?" she asked. "Do we call the state police?"

Sarah stood up, dusted off her hands, and walked her eyes around the kitchen. "We need to talk to this traitor first," she explained. "Maybe we can get a confession out of him?" Sarah rubbed her eyes. "Bonnie, honey, you have to learn to control your temper. This is the second cop you've knocked out cold today...even if this cop deserved it. You're going to get a reputation."

"I'm sorry, Cousin Sarah. I...saw red again," Bonnie apologized. She walked over to Sarah and made a sad face. "I guess I'm a bother, huh?"

Sarah looked into Bonnie's sweet, innocent eyes and felt her heart break. "No, honey, you're not a bother at all," she promised and then tossed a thumb down at Mac. "After all, he's a crook now, not a cop. And I'll bet you a million bucks this is the rat who has been delivering those threatening letters under the door of your toy store."

Bonnie looked at Mac. "I saw Mac around town a few times. I never liked him. He always treated me...rudely," she explained.

"Well," Sarah assured Bonnie, "the only people that rat is going to treat rudely from now on will be his prison friends." Sarah put her eyes on Mac. "Honey, go get me a cup of cold water, okay?"

"Cold water?"

"Cold water," Amanda grinned. "Mr. Corruption is about to have a very icy awakening."

"Oh...I get it," Bonnie said and then, to Sarah's relief, giggled and ran off to the kitchen sink. A minute later she returned with a glass full of icy cold tap water. "Here you go."

Sarah put her gun down on the kitchen table, took the glass of ice water, and bent down. "Time to wake up," she told Mac and threw the water into the fat man's face. Mac's body jerked and then his mouth began to quiver as he sputtered under the water. "Wake up!" Sarah yelled, handed Amanda the glass she was holding, and began slapping Mac across his face a few times. Mac's eyes slowly opened and then closed. "Oh no...wake up!"

Mac opened his eyes again, saw a blurry image of Sarah standing over him, and then he remembered everything he had done to get him to that moment in his life...and then a horrible pain struck his chest. The last thing Mac Newman remembered before dying from a massive heart attack was seeing Sarah's face just enough to cast an image of a beautiful woman into his dying eyes. "Heart...attack..." he managed to whisper. Those were the last words he ever spoke.

"No...no..." Sarah yelled and began doing chest compressions on Mac. "Amanda, you breathe for him."

"No way, love," Amanda cried out and backed away from the kitchen table. "My lips are not touching that man. I'm sorry."

Sarah couldn't blame Amanda for objecting. Mac could have any number of diseases. He had held them at gunpoint just minutes before. Still, her training as a cop kicked in. If the horrible man lived, at least he would face consequences for his crimes. "Bonnie, call 911. Hurry," she ordered as her hands worked frantically to save Mac's life. "Come on...don't die...don't die..." she begged.

Amanda watched Sarah work on Mac and even try to breathe air into the man. "Oh love...don't…"

"I have to try," Sarah explained and breathed more air into Mac's mouth.

"I'll...do the chest compressions," Amanda said, feeling guilt strike her heart. She ran to Mac, dropped down onto her knees, and began working on him.

"Don't die," Sarah pleaded as Amanda worked on Mac's chest.

Bonnie ran to the kitchen phone and dialed 911. "Yes...this is Bonnie Malloy...I need an ambulance at my home...Mac Newman has had a heart attack...yes, the cop, you dum-dum...now get an ambulance over to my house right away." Bonnie slammed down the phone and watched Sarah and Amanda work on Mac. By the time the ambulance arrived, she knew the man was deader than a skunk on the side of a busy highway. "My," she whispered, watching two young paramedics carry Mac out into the snow on a depressing stretcher, "what a day this is turning out to be."

"You said it," Sarah agreed and then took a deep breath of the frigid, snowy air as the hideous snowman that haunted her nightmares laughed at her.

Chapter Ten

Chief Mike Early strolled into the police station wearing a big brown Texas hat that dripped snow down onto his camouflage hunting jacket. Big Chief Mike was a man in his late sixties who carried a little gut and wore his gray mustache so thick it was almost comical. His face, however, wasn't in on the joke and rarely betrayed a smile. "What's all this about Mac having a heart attack during a break-in?" he demanded. "Tony called me back from my hunting trip and I sure ain't happy about it."

Amanda tossed a curious eye at Sarah. "Is this bloke a Yankee or one of those southern people?" she asked.

Sarah eased down behind Tony's desk and slowly folded her arms. "Chief Early?" she asked.

"Mike Early, that's me," Mike stated, looked over at Amanda, and then focused back on Sarah. "But you can call me Big Chief, if you like. Everybody does. And you must be that famous detective woman?"

"My name is Detective Sarah Spencer," Sarah introduced herself.

"My name is Chief Mike Early...Chief of Police," Mike pointed out as if he were spelling a difficult name.

"Are you from the south?" Amanda asked Mike. "I mean, I'm not trying to sound rude, but you don't talk like a Yankee."

"And you don't talk like an American," Mike retorted. He snatched off his cowboy hat and threw it down onto Tony's desk. "What's this about Mac?"

"Well that's...something," Amanda snickered as Mike's bald head came into view. It was very shiny, as if it had been waxed, and shone under the police station lights.

Sarah fought back a grin. She had to admit Mike's shiny head was a little unusual. "Mac Newman died of a massive heart attack earlier today," she explained.

"I told that boy to lay off the donuts," Mike yelled and hid his sorrow by kicking at Tony's desk. "Tony ain't far behind him, either." The chief shook his head. "Mac or Tony wouldn't know a green bean if it jumped up and bit them in the gut. All they understand is sugar and salt. Rest in peace, Mac, but you dug your own grave."

"Yes, it did seem that Mac Newman was extremely overweight and that Tony Massio...could benefit from losing a few pounds," Sarah told Mike in a calm voice.

"A few?" Mike asked and threw his hands up into the air. "Tony isn't fit enough to be a small-town cop and you know it."

Amanda giggled to herself. "I like this bloke," she told Sarah. "He has spunk."

Mike looked at Amanda. "Where are you from? London or Birmingham?"

"London," Amanda told Mike and tipped him a wink.

"My people wouldn't step foot in Birmingham...unless there's a good shop to visit," she joked.

Mike huffed to himself. "My great-grandfather came over on the boat from London. He was an awful drunk who spent his life making shoes, drinking away his earnings, and making sure his family went hungry. How about that for English heritage?" he asked with an ornery squint.

Amanda shrugged her shoulders. "Must have had some Irish in him."

Sarah ducked her head and put her hand over her mouth. "That's not funny!" Mike roared. "My great-grandfather wasn't Irish!"

"And what are you?" Amanda giggled. "Wait...I know...you're called...what is the name I'm looking for, love?" she asked Sarah.

Sarah cleared her throat. "Amanda, honey, I think the name you're searching for is Chief Early," she said and begged Amanda to cool it with her eyes.

"Cheeky bloke is a better name," Amanda replied and plopped down in the chair in front of Tony's desk.

"Chief," Sarah said, "I'm sorry that Mac Newman is dead. However, there is something you need to know—"

"Yes, indeed," Mike informed Sarah in a stern tone. "I want to know why Tony Massio isn't sitting behind that desk. I want to know why he's not getting his fat butt to work and solving his first homicide case. I want to know what you're doing in my town. And I want to know why Bonnie Malloy isn't behind bars."

Sarah calmly clasped her hands together. "Chief Early, Mac Newman held three women at gunpoint earlier today and threatened to kill them."

Mike looked at Sarah with strange eyes. "What are you talking about?" Sarah slowly and calmly explained the events that had transpired inside Bonnie's kitchen. Mike listened with careful ears. "I always knew something wasn't right about that boy. He was sharp as a tack when it came to the book side of police work...but dumber than a lazy cow in a barn when it came to having a lick of common sense." Mike sat down on the edge of Tony's desk. "And what about Tony?" he asked.

"I think Tony is clean," Sarah explained, relieved to see Mike was a smart enough chief of police. "Not very smart...but clean."

Mike rubbed his chin. "You have a good reputation. Talk to me," he demanded.

"I'm here because Bonnie Malloy asked for help. I'm her cousin. I was concerned about the death threats she's been receiving, but now it seems that the murder of Bonnie's boyfriend is a much bigger threat."

"Tony believes Bonnie Malloy killed José Lopez," Mike pointed out.

"Bonnie is innocent," Sarah assured Mike.

"Bonnie is a fruitcake and a sweetheart mixed into one confused mind, but she's not a killer," Amanda added. "That woman would bawl her eyes out if she stepped on a snail unintentionally."

Mike studied Sarah's eyes. "You have an idea who killed José Lopez?"

"Yes," Sarah nodded. "Chief Early—"

"Mike."

"Mike," Sarah continued without missing a beat, "I believe Mayor Mooreland is involved. I also believe Mayor Mooreland is connected to the Solid Grounds land development company, the company José Lopez worked for."

"I knew it!" Mike yelled. He popped to his feet and kicked Tony's desk again. "I knew Mooreland was rotten from the moment I saw him!" Mike pointed a hard finger at Sarah. "You're now deputized as my senior detective. Go arrest Mooreland."

"I wish I could," Sarah told Mike. "I'm afraid I don't have any evidence."

"Get the evidence," Mike demanded.

"Well," Sarah said and stood up, "after Mac Newman's body was taken to the hospital, I visited José Lopez's apartment. His apartment was clean. But," Sarah reached into the front pocket of her coat and pulled out a small plastic bag. "I did find this."

Mike eyed the plastic bag. "I don't see anything."

"There's a single contact lens in this bag," Sarah explained and gently pointed out the location of the small, rubbery circle. "Amanda found this on the kitchen floor of Jose's apartment...by chance rather than skill, I might add."

"I dropped a French fry on the kitchen floor," Amanda jumped in. "When I reached down to pick it up, I spotted the contact lens near the stove. Who says playing with your food doesn't pay off?"

Mike rubbed his chin again. "Okay, so we have a contact lens. The lens could belong to José Lopez's killer. Or to Lopez himself."

"I already contacted Dr. Green," Sarah continued. "Dr. Green confirmed that José Lopez didn't wear any form of eyewear." Sarah walked over to the office window and looked out at a heavy falling snow covering a very dark night. "I checked Jose's apartment. Everything was tidy, in order, and very neat."

"Which means?" Mike asked.

Sarah kept her eyes on the darkness. "Bonnie Malloy said she was invited to the apartment for dinner before José was murdered," she told Mike in a clear voice. "Bonnie claims that the apartment seemed as if it was not being lived in."

"I'm growing gray hairs here, Detective. Get to the point," Mike fussed.

"I don't believe José Lopez lived in Four Ridges at all," Sarah explained. "The clothes I found in his apartment looked brand new...the dishes...the furniture, everything."

Mike walked behind Tony's desk and sat down. "Which means?"

"Bonnie's death threats—"

"Yeah, I know all about the letters," Mike assured Sarah. "So what?"

"José Lopez worked for Solid Grounds Land Development Company, Mike." Sarah turned away from the window, walked over to Tony's desk, picked up a brown cup of coffee, and took a sip. "I believe José Lopez was sent to Four Ridges to ensure Bonnie Malloy vacated her toy store, one way or the other."

"You mean he was sent here to kill her?"

"If the threatening letters Mac Newman was delivering to the toy store didn't work...yes," Sarah nodded.

"Mac was delivering those letters? How do you know that?" Mike demanded.

"A hunch," Sarah confessed. "No proof...just a cop and her gut." Sarah folded her arms. "We should check the paper, the pens, the handwriting...but I have a good hunch it will be a match for Mac Newman. Mike, when I returned from dropping Tony off at his apartment earlier, I found this police station empty. Mac was nowhere in sight. However, Mr. Branch, the man who owns the diner, said Mac Newman stopped by for lunch and before he left, he had the lunch crowd believing Bonnie Malloy was guilty of murder. But we'll get back to Mac in a minute. First—"

Before Sarah could finish her sentence a hard knock struck at the office door.

"Yeah, what?" Mike roared. "I'm in a meeting!"

"This is Mayor Mooreland. I demand we speak at once."

Mike looked up at Sarah. Sarah skillfully grabbed Amanda out of the chair she was sitting in and backed them up to the office window. "Keep your hand in your coat pocket, right on your gun," she whispered to Amanda.

"Got it, love," Amanda whispered back, feeling her stomach become tense.

"If Mayor Mooreland is alone, then ease off, but if he has someone with him, stay prepared."

"Being your best friend is never easy," Amanda whispered in a quick voice as Mike got up to answer the door. Sarah quickly reached into her coat pocket and rested her hand on a gun that was prepared for battle.

"What is it, Mayor?" Mike asked. "I'm in a serious meeting."

Mayor Mooreland glanced past Mike and spotted Sarah and Amanda. "Where is Detective Massio?"

"On assignment," Mike explained in a gruff voice.

Mayor Mooreland eased the office door open with a wooden cane. "Detective Spencer, how nice to finally meet you in person," he said in a cold voice as a large man built like a tank stepped up next to him. Amanda glanced at Sarah with worried eyes. "I heard the tragic news about Officer Newman and came to inquire about his death."

Sarah narrowed her eyes and studied the man standing beside Mayor Mooreland. The man sported a military haircut and a black suit...normal gear for a hired gun. "Mac Newman died of a massive heart attack."

"Oh, that is tragic," Mayor Mooreland said in a polite yet slithery voice that made Sarah sick to her stomach. "I suppose we will have to honor Officer Newman in some form, right, Chief Early?"

"I ain't so sure," Mike told Mayor Mooreland. "I have a credible source that has informed me the man was on the take."

Mayor Mooreland struck his eyes at Sarah. "Is that so?" he asked. "My, that is awful news. Officer Newman seemed...decent."

Mike eased back to Tony's desk. "Looks can be very deceiving," he informed Mayor Mooreland in a voice that displeased the old man. "Now, if you don't mind, I'm in a meeting."

Mayor Mooreland rested his wooden cane on the floor. "Where are we at concerning the José Lopez case?" he asked in a stern voice.

"Man was found dead just this morning. Murder cases take a while," Mike explained.

Mayor Mooreland struck his eyes at Sarah again. "How nice it must be to have such an experienced homicide detective in town," he said in a cold voice. "Very...convenient, as well."

"I don't question gold nuggets kicked up by wandering feet," Mike told Mayor Mooreland. "Detective Spencer arrived in town to help her cousin Bonnie Malloy. That's just fine with me. As a matter of fact, I just put her in charge of this case."

Mayor Mooreland snapped his eyes at Mike. "You do not have the authority—"

"Look," Mike boldly interrupted, "a man is dead and I'm going to find out who killed him."

"You were supposed to be on a two-week sabbatical," Mayor Mooreland pointed out. "Perhaps it would be wise if you returned to your sabbatical."

"Are you threatening me?" Mike roared. The hired gun standing beside Mayor Moorland stepped forward. "I'll slap cuffs on you if I have to," Mike promised the guy.

Mayor Mooreland held up his left hand. "Chief," he said, "I was simply implying that perhaps it would be wise to allow Tony Massio to continue working on the case."

"Tony doesn't have the brain cells to fart straight," Mike snapped. "Detective Spencer is my woman."

Mayor Mooreland studied Sarah and then looked down at her hand. The woman was clearly prepared for a fight. "I have to disagree and clearly state that it will be a pleasure when Willis LaPorte takes over your job."

"Willis LaPorte, that spineless hippie who ran off to Canada instead of fighting in Vietnam?"

"Be that as it may," Mayor Mooreland replied, gritting his teeth, "he is the correct man for the job." Mayor Mooreland glanced around Tony's office. "Four Ridges is my town now, is that clear? I'm in control. I will put my people in place and get rid of...the dead weight, so to speak."

Mike stepped up to Mayor Mooreland. "Get out of here before I send you flying."

"Don't threaten me," Mayor Mooreland hissed and then looked at Sarah. "It seems that I am being forced to play rougher than needed. So be it."

"Tell your pals at the Solid Grounds Land Development Company that I'm going to arrest every last one of them if that's what it takes to get to the bottom of this case," Sarah told Mayor Mooreland, a little uneasy about the sudden change in his behavior. Mayor Mooreland was all but confessing that he had had José killed and that he would kill anyone that dared step into his path. "And by the way, it's a shame that Mac Newman didn't get a chance to run me out of town like you ordered him to do."

"I don't know what you're talking about," Mayor Mooreland told Sarah in an icy tone and then looked at her with deadly eyes. "Perhaps I will have to find out. Goodnight."

Sarah watched Mayor Mooreland and his hired gun vanish down the dark corridor and out of sight. "Mike?" she asked.

"Yeah?" Mike kicked the office door closed.

"I'm not sure who killed José Lopez, but what I do know is that he was just a small fish sacrificed to appease some pretty big sharks." Sarah looked at Amanda. "This is serious, honey. Ready for war?"

Amanda sighed. "Love, I've been shot at, chased, and choked...I've even been infected with a deadly virus...what's a sour old prune of a mayor compared to all that?"

Outside in the snow, Mayor Mooreland snatched out his cell phone and made a call. "We have trouble," he said through gritted teeth and prepared to make Sarah eat her words.

Chapter Eleven

"Notice anything about the hired gun?" Sarah asked Mike.

Amanda threw her hand up into the air and began waiving it around like an excited schoolgirl. "I know...oh please...pick me, love...I know the answer!"

"The pretty lady in the front," Sarah said in a proud voice.

"Yes, I'll take observations for four hundred dollars, Alex. Glasses...he was wearing glasses!" Amanda blurted out and then grinned. "This pretty lady is becoming a real cop. Thank you."

Mike rolled his eyes. Amanda was silly but he liked her. "Yeah, yeah, I noticed the guy wearing glasses and immediately thought about the missing contact lens. I didn't say a word because I figured you two noticed the same deal."

Sarah began to speak but stopped when Tony stumbled into his office wearing a white bandage around his head. "Chief," he said in a pained voice, shook snow off his trench coat, and then looked at Sarah and Amanda. "Where is Bonnie Malloy?" he asked in a careful voice.

"At a friend's house, for safety reasons," Sarah confirmed.

Tony let out a sigh of relief. "I figured I better make an appearance, with Mac being dead and all," he told Mike.

"I'm honored," Mike told Tony in a sarcastic voice. "Just imagine a man actually earning his paycheck by doing honest work? That's unheard of, Detective Massio."

Tony winced. "I didn't mean to be put out of action. Bonnie Malloy assaulted me today."

"And just how did you let Bonnie Malloy get close enough to clobber you, boy?"

"I…well…Chief, she had a weapon—"

"A wooden candy cane," Sarah quickly pointed out.

"A weapon is a weapon," Tony insisted.

"And just how did Bonnie Malloy manage to smack you with a wooden candy cane?" Mike yelled at Tony and then shook his head. "You're going to give me an ulcer, boy!"

"Chief, I've been handling the murder case with professionalism," Tony said in a defensive tone that sounded more like a whine. "You can check the case file. All the i's are dotted and all the t's are crossed. You should be proud."

Mike rubbed his bald head. "Tony, you and Mac are book smart, I give you that. But when it comes to having common sense, you're as dry as a jellyfish in the desert." Mike tossed a thumb at Sarah. "Detective Spencer is in charge. You take orders from her," he continued. "And if you had been here a few minutes ago you would have been privy to a very important spectacle."

"I saw Mayor Mooreland leaving when I arrived," Tony told Mike. "I figured he—"

"Mooreland is corrupt," Mike snapped at Tony. "Did you know that?"

"No." Tony began biting on his thumb nail.

"You still think Bonnie Malloy is the guilty one?"

"Okay...okay," Tony said. "So, maybe I might be wrong. Maybe Mayor Mooreland did have something to with José Lopez's death." Tony sat down on the edge of his desk. The desk creaked under his weight. "I've been at home thinking... after I got my head checked out...and it occurred to me to check out the company that built the new town hall."

Sarah looked at Tony, impressed. "And?" she asked.

Tony stopped biting his thumb nail. "I called Natalie Strauss—"

"Old Chicken Legs?" Mike asked.

"Natalie is the town clerk," Tony pointed out for Sarah's benefit.

"One ugly town clerk...but continue, detective."

Tony focused on Sarah. "Natalie did some checking for me and told me that Solid Grounds Development subcontracted a company called Fallwell Construction to build the new town hall. I jumped online and did some checking, and guess what?"

"What?" Mike asked and then barked, "Get to the point before I end up in a nursing home!"

Tony winced. "Fallwell Construction is located in Detroit and owned by Senator Robert Kallerson."

Mike let out a heavy, angry grumble. "Kallerson is a crook!"

"Senator Kallerson also supports a radical activist group that has its claws dug into the European Union," Tony explained. "Senator Kallerson supports open borders without restrictions and has managed to swindle millions of taxpayer dollars and funnel that money to the group he supports." Tony felt pride rise in his chest and his chubby cheeks pinked up. "Senator Kallerson is known for his communist ideas and...distaste for American values. He was voted into office because of some very radical people live in Michigan...people with lots and lots of greenbacks in their deep pockets."

"Kallerson has been attempting to change the landscape of Michigan for the last four years," Mike complained. "Now, I don't mind immigrants coming to America. I'm all for folks wanting a better life...the right and legal way. If folks are willing to enter our country illegally, how can we trust they're gonna mind our laws or respect our culture? America has enough problems without adding to them by allowing illegal criminals to leapfrog our laws." Mike stood up and rubbed his sore back. "I don't care if a billion people from...Japan or Mexico or Russia...want to immigrate to America, just as long as they do it legally." Mike made a sick face. "Kallerson is constantly spitting on our laws and trying to make Michigan into some kind of safe harbor for illegal immigrants."

"Kallerson needs the votes," Tony added. "He only won the last election by a two percent lead."

Sarah took a second to soak in all the information Tony was throwing into the air. "Tony, do you know who owns Solid Grounds Development?" she asked.

Tony beamed a proud smile. "A man named Patrick Capps. And guess what? Patrick Capps is Mrs. Mooreland's brother."

"Now we're getting somewhere," Mike said and hit Tony's desk. "Maybe you do have common sense, boy. It's a shame you don't use your brain more often."

Sarah walked up to Tony and patted his shoulder. "Good work, Detective Massio."

Tony felt his cheeks begin to burn. "The internet is a useful tool," he explained and then looked around the office. "I guess Mayor Mooreland could be connected to José Lopez's murder, then. My research seems to prove that there are some very...curious...links."

Mike grabbed his cowboy hat and tossed it on his bald head. "I need some coffee. I'm heading to the diner. I'll be right back."

Sarah watched Mike storm out of the office. "Tony," she said in a careful voice, "I went to José Lopez's apartment and had a look around. I found this." Tony watched Sarah pull out the plastic bag holding the contact lens. "Amanda found a contact lens on the floor."

Tony squinted his eyes and then rubbed his sore head. "I'll take your word for it."

Sarah put the bag away and bit down on her lip. "Did you see anyone leaving with Mayor Mooreland when you arrived?"

"No," Tony shook his head. "All I saw was the mayor's car pulling away when I arrived."

"Okay," Sarah said and began pacing back and forth. "I think it's time we get back out into the cold," she explained. "Tony, I want you to watch Mayor Mooreland's house. Amanda and I are going to watch the town hall."

"A stakeout?" Tony asked in an excited voice. Sarah nodded yes.

"Great!" Tony exclaimed and then asked in a quick voice, "Can I have my car back? I had to borrow my neighbor's old Mazda to drive here."

Sarah reached into her coat pocket, grabbed out the keys to Tony's Oldsmobile, and tossed them to the man. "Amanda and I will drive the SUV I rented," she explained and then focused on Tony. "Listen to me, Detective Massio," she said in a serious, almost pleading voice, "the hired gun that showed up with Mayor Mooreland tonight was wearing glasses. Glasses are out of character for a scumbag like that. Do you understand what I'm saying?"

Tony didn't exactly understand. "So what? He's an egghead, or what?" he began to say and then paused as his eyes widened with realization. He looked for all the world like a bright neon DUH! sign had started blinking over his head. "The contact lens you found?"

Sarah nodded yes. "I believe the hired gun that showed up with Mayor Mooreland tonight is the person who killed José Lopez. Maybe he was wearing glasses because he lost his contact lens."

"And José Lopez worked for Solid Grounds Land Development Company," Tony said. "Mrs. Mooreland's brother owns Solid Grounds and Senator Kallerson owns the Fallwell Construction Company." Tony rubbed his chin. "This case is really starting to piece together."

"We have assumptions but no evidence," Sarah pointed out in a troubled voice. "Tony, right now Mayor Mooreland is desperate to prevent the truth from getting out and will take any desperate measures needed to ensure victory for his cause."

"And that means killing all of us," Amanda pointed out. "So listen, Mr. Roly-Poly, you better be extra careful tonight, because the wolves are out roaming."

Tony yanked out his gun and checked the clip. "Anyone who stands in my way tonight will get a mouth full of lead," he said, struggling to sound like a real tough guy. "I've been waiting for a moment like this all my life. I finally get to be in on the action...no more writing stupid traffic tickets to grandmas who drove two miles over the speed limit...making coffee for arrogant cops who laugh at me behind my back...this is the big time, and Tony Massio is going to make a name for himself."

"Listen, my fine friend," Amanda said cautiously, "I hate to bust your bubble, but a woman slapped you upside the head with a wooden candy cane today and knocked you out cold. I would stop the Clint Eastwood act if I were you and worry about not showing my butt crack to the enemy."

Tony nervously patted at the white bandage wrapped around his head. "Okay, so a killer got a lucky swing, big deal," he snapped at Amanda. "That doesn't mean a man sticks his head into the sand, does it?"

"You better never call me a killer again," a harsh voice exploded.

Tony spun around and saw Bonnie standing in the office doorway. "What are you doing here?"

"I got lonely," Bonnie explained and looked at Sarah with wide, tremulous eyes. "I also got really scared. Melanie is a sweet woman but she...farts a lot. I guess old women do that."

Sarah was actually very happy to see Bonnie. "Cousin Bonnie," she explained, "you're going to stay in my eyesight for the rest of the night, okay?"

Bonnie's face exploded with joy. She ran to Sarah, grabbed the poor woman, and began swinging her around and around. "Oh, this is so much fun!" she cried. "I was hoping you wouldn't be mad at me and you're not!"

"Bonnie...honey...my ribs...can't...breathe," Sarah cried out in pain.

Amanda quickly ran to Sarah's rescue, pried Bonnie loose,

and sighed. "Love, you're going to force us to start wearing body armor."

"Sorry," Bonnie said with a giggle. "I'm just so excited. I mean...it's sad that that awful Mac Newman person had to die...but this is like being trapped in a really neat Nancy Drew mystery. The snow...it's nighttime...and..." Bonnie's mind immediately switched tracks. The glowing joy and excitement in her eyes dimmed and tears began to appear. "Oh José...my sweet señor...come back to Momma...my darling chili pepper—"

"Chile pepper?" Tony asked and rolled his eyes. "That's a little...much."

"No...no..." Sarah begged Tony.

"Too late," Amanda whimpered, watching a dark cloud cover Bonnie's eyes. "Incoming!"

Bonnie spun around and charged at Tony. Tony let out a cry and tried to run but Bonnie tackled him down onto the office floor and began beating him in the head with her mittens. "I'll show you...I'll show you!" she screamed.

Mike stepped into the office doorway holding a cup of coffee and watched Bonnie go to town on Tony. "It's like having the circus in town," he told Sarah and Amanda, took a sip of his coffee, and then barked in a loud voice, "On your feet!"

Bonnie jerked her head up, looked into a pair of mean bulldog eyes, and scrambled to her feet. "He started it!"

Tony wiped a trail of blood away from his nose. "Did not!"

Mike rubbed his forehead. "If I had any hair it would all fall out right about now," he griped and then locked eyes with Tony. "On your feet, Detective. We have work to do." Tony slowly stood up and looked at Sarah and Amanda with embarrassed eyes. "I heard you talking about a stakeout," Mike told Sarah. "I'll ride with Detective Massio and cover Mooreland's house. You take the...linebacker woman...and cover the town hall. If nothing occurs during the night, we'll meet back here at oh-seven hundred."

"What time?" Bonnie asked.

"Seven in the morning, love," Amanda explained.

"Oh...why didn't you just say so?" Bonnie asked Mike. "And people call me stupid?"

Mike rolled his eyes. "Somebody arrest her," he mumbled under his breath. "If one of our teams encounters trouble during the night, call for backup ASAP. Is that clear? I don't want any heroics, and that includes you," Mike pointed at Sarah. "You may be a celebrity cop, but this is my town and we're going to do things by the book."

"Yes, sir," Sarah assured Mike. "I have no want or desire to be a hero. As a matter of fact, I was never a hero...just...blessed —" Sarah stopped talking when she heard the cell phone in her coat pocket ring. She snatched out the cell phone and checked the incoming call. "It's Pete," she said in a relieved voice. "I need to take this call. It's very important." Sarah walked over to the office window and answered the call. "What do you have for me, Pete?"

Pete shoved a half-smoked cigar into his mouth and locked his eyes onto the brown folder he held. "Kiddo, I don't know how you manage to always shake up a hornet's nest, but you do," he grumbled.

"It must be bad."

"Bad isn't the word for it," Pete informed Sarah. "Kiddo, we're talking about murder...gun running...drugs...human trafficking...political   sabotage...blackmail...media manipulation...you name it and this guy Patrick Capps has his hands into it."

"Patrick Capps own the Solid Grounds Land Development Company," Sarah told Pete.

"He owns quite a few land development companies," Pete pointed out and spit his cigar out. "And two guesses who his silent partner might be?"

"Mayor Mooreland."

"You got it," Pete told Sarah. "Kiddo, you're in a mess." Pete drew in a tired breath, glanced at a box of half-eaten Chinese food on his desk, and then went to work telling Sarah about how Patrick Capps and his brother-in-law were connected to a covert agency operating out of the United Nations, working to irreparably damage the physical and political landscape of America. "They attack small towns, kiddo, while all the other greedy politicians are focused on the bigger cities..."

"Well, we've got our work cut out for us," Sarah said grimly when she finally hung up the phone with Pete. "Chief...Tony...let's do this stakeout before it's too late."

Chapter Twelve

The falling snow covered the toy store with heavy, icy hands roaming a dark and deadly night filled with murderous intent. Sarah felt this shadow lurking inside each snowflake that dropped down from the night sky, covering her eyes the way Bonnie's sudden episodes seemed to cover her eyes. "Anyone have a good story to tell?" she asked, standing beside a window and peering out toward the town hall.

Amanda plopped down on a wooden stool painted like a gum drop and searched the dark toy store. Suddenly all the cozy and fun toys seemed to have transformed into creepy little monsters on their wooden shelves, peering at her with angry, beady little plastic eyes that were somehow alive. "Can't we turn on at least one light, Los Angeles?" she asked Sarah and then shivered all over. "It's so creepy in here."

Bonnie didn't mind the dark. She sat on the front counter swinging her legs like a happy child enjoying a warm summer day. "Oh, you can't be afraid of the dark, sweetie," she told Amanda. "Why, over there...that big shadow...is just my train.

And over there," Bonnie pointed to the massive shadowy form, "is just the dollhouse I bought from a woman in Tennessee."

Amanda wanted to tell Bonnie that darkness changes innocence into horror but bit her tongue. "See anything?" she asked Sarah.

"The town hall is still dark," Sarah said and began wondering if Mike and Tony were having better luck—and then began worrying that if they were...would they somehow mess up the entire case? A cop had to trust his or her fellow cops. But still, Sarah worried, could she trust a bald-headed Texan living in Michigan and a Los Angeles reject? "That's mean," she whispered, "Mike is a good man and Tony...is learning."

"What, love?" Amanda asked.

"Nothing, June Bug," Sarah sighed. "Why don't you take over for me? I want to go look around the storage room again."

"In the dark...creepy," Amanda said, feeling the darkness laughing at her.

Sarah turned away from the window, helped Amanda off the stool, and then looked toward Bonnie. "Flashlight?"

"Oh sure," Bonnie beamed. She quickly jumped down to the floor and hurried behind the wooden counter. "Let's see...oh yeah..." Bonnie ducked her head down and began searching the bottom shelf. "Here it is!" she exclaimed, reached into a wooden box, and pulled out a peppermint-striped flashlight. "Want me to test the batteries?"

"No," Sarah answered in a quick voice. "Honey, we're in blackout mode, okay? No lights. Can't let anyone know we're in here."

"Oh...okay," Bonnie replied in a cheerful voice and handed Sarah the flashlight. "I can make us some more coffee?"

"Sure, honey," Sarah smiled, tossed Amanda a tired eye through the darkness, and wandered away toward the storage room. "Okay...we have the killer possibly identified...we have the guilty parties under a bright light...now, how to wrap them into a net?" she asked herself, walking into the dark storage room. The air in the storage room smelled of dust, wood, cold and...and...Sarah paused. Someone was in the storage room. She smelled the faint scent of cologne. "I'll just take a quick look around," she called out over her shoulder and then eased back into the toy store. "Looks clear. I'll take over at the window again," she said in a loud voice and closed the door with quick hands, yanked out her gun, and let her mind go to work. "José must have given the code to Mayor Mooreland once he manipulated Bonnie into giving it to him...it sure can't be Mayor Mooreland in the storage room." She immediately thought of the mayor's glasses-wearing henchman and her blood ran cold all over again.

Sarah studied the storage room door and waited. Silence fell. Only the sound of freezing, angry, howling winds touched her ears—well, that and the sound of Bonnie singing a song as she made coffee. "What to do?" Sarah wondered, feeling her stomach tighten with anxiety. The hired gun she had seen with Mayor Mooreland wasn't the type of man she could beat up with a broom or out-shoot in a gun fight. The hired muscle she saw appeared to be a professional killer, extremely skilled at his work. "He must have snuck in here using the code..." Sarah paused and studied the darkness. "Before we arrived? That has to be the case, because Bonnie reactivated the alarm when we arrived."

Sarah felt her thoughts turn to Mike and Tony. She quickly pulled her cell phone out and made a call. "Mike? it's Detective Spencer...I have an intruder in the storage room," she whispered. "I believe it's Mayor Mooreland's hired gun...what? How many cars...no, no, I understand...you need to keep watch there, something important could be happening...I'll...handle the intruder."

Sarah ended the call, put her cell phone away, and looked at the storage room door. *I'm hiding in the dark, Sarah...gonna get you...Boo! Gonna get you and your dreams of having a baby...hiding in the dark...waiting in the darkness...* Sarah saw a hideous snowman slithering around in the storage room, going from box to box, hissing and growling, waiting for her—daring her—to enter his world. Sarah closed her eyes and tried to think. "I'm...scared," she whispered. "Death is inside that room...what do I do?" Before a confident thought could enter Sarah's heart, she heard movement come from inside the storage room. She froze and listened to the silence. "Moving...toward the door," she whispered and quickly dropped down onto one knee and aimed her gun at the storage room door.

Jimmy "the Hawk" Leque, a hired mercenary who had served in the Canadian military as a sniper, was through waiting. It was time to kill his. He had listened to the three women talking in the front room for long enough. Nothing the women said was useful or beneficial. What mattered—the true danger—was that Sarah Spencer and her team of idiot cops knew too much. The old man should have let Lopez live and killed the stupid cow, he thought, stalking through the darkness toward the storage room door wearing his special forces night vision goggles. "Killing Lopez was foolish." Jimmy stopped for a second, checked his Glock 19, and then visualized the front room. The layout of the toy store was burned into his memory. Jimmy had every square inch of the toy store memorized. However, he warned himself, killing three women wasn't going to be simple. The cop would surely put up a fight, which meant she had to die first. The woman from London would take the second bullet and the Malloy woman would take the third bullet. "Fast, swift and clean," Jimmy whispered. "Clean and swift."

Sarah felt her heart begin racing. Why was she so scared? "Focus," she whispered as sweat began to pour down her face, aiming her gun at the storage room door. "He's going to attack and there's no room for hesitation. You'll get one shot." Sarah closed her eyes for a second and saw the old man again, with his soothing voice. *Now, you have to stop being so careful, girl,* the old man told Sarah, sitting on a wooden chair and whittling a piece of wood with an old pocketknife. His eyes gazed across the warm field of sunflowers. *Why, you and Pete were a good team. You were never afraid with Pete at your side.* "Pete isn't here," Sarah told the old man in a miserable voice. "I'm sick of fighting the snowman."

Now is that any way to talk? Sure ain't, the old man told Sarah in a stern voice. He raised his wise eyes and made Sarah look into his wrinkled face as a warm breeze touched the straw hat he was wearing. *That boy inside that room done made a mistake and you know it. You have the upper hand. Now stop spooking yourself.*

"My baby...I want to have my baby...if I die...we both die," Sarah nearly cried. "Why can't I be at peace? Why does the snowman keep chasing me?"

You created that monster...only you can kill it.

"I tried."

Keep trying and stop being so careful because you're liable to get yourself killed. Just be a...cop, girl.

"I'm so tired..."

You ain't even to the last round, girl. You best get your second wind and handle yourself, the old man warned Sarah and motioned out at the sunflowers with his pocketknife. *You can't be where I'm at until you win the last round. Now stop being careful or you're going to get yourself killed!*

Sarah's eyes flung open just as the door leading into the storage room began to creep open. "Careful...stop being careful..." she whispered and then, to her own shock, shot to her feet, charged at the storage room door, and kicked it as hard as she possibly could. She caught her breath as the realization ripped through her mind, "I need him alive...not dead!"

The door Jimmy was opening suddenly crashed backward into his body. Completely taken off guard, he lost his balance and stumbled backward, tripped on a nearby box, and toppled down onto the floor. As he did, the light to the storage room flicked on. Jimmy snapped his head up just in time to see Sarah drop down onto one knee and aim her gun at him. "Freeze!" Sarah yelled. "One move and you're a dead man!"

Rage filled Jimmy's mind. How had this stupid woman managed to get the best of him? Jimmy had killed many men and now he was at the mercy of a cop? No way. Never. He let out a growl, kicked the box toward Sarah, and tried a roll and shoot maneuver. Sarah didn't hesitate. She fired off two bullets before Jimmy could get to a decent firing position. One bullet tore into Jimmy's firing hand and the second struck his right shoulder. Jimmy let out a vicious scream as his gun went flying down onto the floor and the wound in his hand began gushing blood.

"I said don't move!" Sarah yelled.

"You're dead!" Jimmy yelled back, grabbed his wounded hand, and then noticed his shoulder wasn't faring much better. "You're messing with the wrong business, lady! You've just signed your death warrant. You may take me down, but they'll come for you. And they have more power and money than you can imagine. They'll chase you to the ends of the earth…" He stopped and gasped, clutching his shoulder in intense pain.

Amanda appeared behind Sarah, breathing hard and scared to death. "Love…" she asked in a shaky voice and then spotted Jimmy lying on the floor. "Oh my."

Sarah glanced back at Amanda and saw her best friend holding a gun. "If he moves…shoot him," she told Amanda, eased forward, and kicked Jimmy's gun toward the back door. "Okay, it's time we talk."

"I'd rather drop dead."

"Okay," Sarah said, aimed her gun at Jimmy's chest, and began to squeeze the trigger.

Jimmy couldn't believe his eyes. Was the stupid woman cop really going to kill him? Cops were supposed to be the good guys…well, most cops, anyway. Jimmy had run into his share of cops that couldn't be bought or intimidated, and Sarah, he knew, was one of those cops. But now the woman was actually going to fill him full of lead. "Wait…wait…" he yelled and raised his good hand up into the air, "don't shoot."

"Did you kill José Lopez?" Sarah demanded.

Jimmy licked his lips, hating himself for allowing a cop to trick him. "Yeah, I killed José Lopez. I injected him with an untraceable poison, then shoved his body into this room, put a knife in his back, and left."

"Why?" Sarah asked.

"José Lopez was a hired stooge, like me," Jimmy informed Sarah. "His job was to talk Bonnie Malloy into vacating while Mac Newman pressured her through a series of threatening letters. Mr. Mooreland didn't want any bloodshed. When it became clear that Bonnie Malloy wasn't going to vacate, the order was given to kill Bonnie Malloy. José Lopez objected...the man was spineless. A real sap. He thought we should keep trying. Mr. Mooreland decided to kill him instead and use his death to get rid of Bonnie Malloy." Jimmy shook his head in disgust. "The old man should have killed Bonnie and let José live."

"What? Kill me?"

Jimmy looked past Sarah and Amanda and saw a very angry Bonnie clutching a wooden candy cane with white knuckles. Bonnie burst into the storage room, charged forward, and began beating Jimmy over the head with the wooden candy cane like a raging bull. "You killed my sweet señor...why?" Bonnie screamed as she beat Jimmy senseless.

"Bonnie!" Sarah screamed and desperately struggled to pull Bonnie away from Jimmy. The woman was fiercely powerful and, for some reason, Sarah couldn't pull her away from Jimmy...not even one inch. "Amanda, help me!"

Amanda grabbed Bonnie's arm, but Bonnie threw her to the side. "Why did you kill my sweet señor?" she screamed at Jimmy as the man tried to use his good hand to block the wooden candy cane. To his shock—and horror—the woman was extremely powerful. "Why did you kill José?" Bonnie screamed as the dark cloud filled her vicious eyes. "Why?"

Bonnie swung the wooden candy cane back into the air, kicked Jimmy's good hand away with a powerful boot, and then smacked the man so hard in the head that the wooden stick broke in half. Jimmy saw stars...and then darkness.

"Bonnie," Sarah moaned and finally managed to drag her cousin out of the storage room. "Up front...now," she ordered.

"My sweet señor," Bonnie said like a dog getting in one last growl and then walked away into the darkness.

Sarah watched Bonnie vanish and then ran back to Amanda. "I think Ms. Mood Swings killed him," Amanda told Sarah in a worried voice. "Look at his head...there's blood."

Sarah quickly secured Jimmy's hands behind his back with a pair of handcuffs and began to stand up. As she did, something caught on the palm of her hand. Just as she went to wipe her hand off, she looked at her palm and realized what it was. "A contact lens?" she told Amanda and studied the night vision goggles covering Jimmy's face. "Oh. Hey, June Bug?"

"Yes, love?" Amanda asked.

"I think I know how to catch the biggest fish in the pond," Sarah explained, stood up, and backed away from Jimmy. "But boy, spending a fun-filled day shopping in O'Mally's sounds really great right about now."

"What would our lives be without a little murder...danger...and bad guys," Amanda asked and then hugged Sarah's arm. "I have a feeling the roller coaster has just reached the top of the first hill, right love?"

"I'm afraid so," Sarah nodded and looked down at Jimmy. It was time to make her next move on the chessboard. It was also time to stop being careful and start playing by a set of rules that only madmen understood.

Chapter Thirteen

Jimmy opened his eyes, groggy and struggling to shake the sleep out of his eyelids. His mind blurred, disoriented. His head felt as if someone had taken an ax to it. "What..." he mumbled.

"Wake up," Sarah ordered.

Jimmy raised his eyes and spotted Sarah's blurry face. "What..." he said again, trying to focus. The blurriness attacking his vision was familiar—not the type of blurriness a person suffered after being bonked on the head. "Hey, where are my glasses?"

Sarah took her right boot and kicked a black bag she had found hidden behind a pile of boxes. The black bag held Jimmy's field supplies along with his eyeglasses. The night vision goggles that Jimmy had been wearing were advanced and very high tech—the goggles also had a special pair of lenses to compensate for Jimmy's prescription. "Looking for this?" Sarah asked.

Jimmy spotted a blurry black shape. "My field bag," he

said and tried to reach for the black bag. That was when he noticed his hands were handcuffed behind his back. "Let me go…"

Sarah watched Jimmy struggle to free his hands. "You're trapped," Sarah explained.

Jimmy let out a vicious growl and struggled up to a sitting position. "You're a dead woman," he threatened Sarah, even though he couldn't see her face. That was when Amanda appeared and slapped his eyeglasses on. Sarah's beautiful face became crystal clear.

"Shut up and listen to the boss lady or I'll…kick you in the leg," Amanda warned Jimmy and quickly backed over to Sarah.

Sarah put her boot on the black bag. "While you were unconscious, I came up with a little plan, but decided to change it after I found your bag."

"You searched my bag?"

"Yes, I did," Sarah nodded. "I found some very interesting items, including your cell phone, which had some very…damaging text messages from a certain Senator Kallerson."

Jimmy gritted his teeth at Sarah. "Kallerson is going to have you killed. Mark my words."

"Maybe…maybe not." Sarah shrugged her shoulders. "Right now, the ball is in your court. You see, I have these." Sarah pulled a plastic bag from her coat pocket. "Inside this bag are your contact lens. You are missing them, aren't you?"

Anger and anxiety filled Jimmy's mind. "Where did you find those? Those are new…but they irritate my eyes. I'm having to constantly take them out and rinse my eyes," he explained and then closed his eyes. He flashed back to when he'd lost one of the lenses just a few days ago…his cruel hands shoved José up against the refrigerator in that miserable, empty rented apartment José was calling home. When Jimmy pushed José against the refrigerator, José flailed around and one of his hands hit Jimmy's eye. Out came the contact lens. In the rush to inject him with the poison, he'd never found it. To make matters worse, the second contact lens fell out while Jimmy was dragging Jose's dead body into the storage room of the toy store. Disgusted and fed up, Jimmy had taken to wearing his back-up glasses until he could acquire a new set of contact lenses.

"Two boxes of those lenses were inside my black bag."

"I know," Sarah nodded. "And I'm sure those prescription contact lenses with your name on them will match the lenses that we found…one at José Lopez's apartment and one right inside this room. I'm sure a jury will find that very interesting. After all, you confessed to killing José Lopez, but I'm sure Mr. Mooreland or Mr. Capps or Senator Kallerson has you covered legally, right? Sure, they do, which means right now it's your word against mine—"

"And mine," Amanda added and gave Jimmy a skunk eye.

Sarah patted Amanda's hand. "And yours, honey," she agreed. "A cop needs evidence and I seem to have found the evidence I need to make a jury cast a very ugly eye at you. However," Sarah emphasized, "the contact lens alone might not be enough. Good thing the text messages on your phone will add a cherry to the whole sundae, don't you think? And I'm assuming that Senator Kallerson will not be too pleased to see his private messages made public."

"Are you kidding?" Amanda asked. "The media will have a field day. Besides, they don't even care who's innocent or guilty

—" Amanda stopped talking and looked into Sarah's pleading eyes. "Oh, sorry love...my lips ran away with me for a second."

"You're both dead," Jimmy threatened.

"And so are you, unless you agree to assist me," Sarah warned.

"Help you? You're out of your mind!"

Sarah tossed a thumb toward the storage room door. "Bonnie, honey?"

A shadowy figure appeared wearing a blue ski coat, red ski pants, and a hockey mask. "You rang?" Bonnie asked and began thunking a hockey stick against her left palm. "Is this guy giving you lip again?"

"Maybe you should teach this skunk to be more...helpful," Sarah told Bonnie and stepped backward a few feet. "Careful, June Bug, I have a feeling this is going to get very ugly."

Bonnie glared at Jimmy and began walking toward him. "Time to play with the beaver," she growled.

"Wolf...wolf, love," Amanda whispered.

"Oh yeah...wolf," Bonnie corrected herself. She lifted the hockey stick up into the air and prepared to take a swing at Jimmy.

Jimmy, although he was a deadly killer, wasn't keen on the idea of getting beaten black and blue with a hockey stick. Besides, this woman looked more than capable of hefting quite a blow. "Hey...back off..."

Bonnie narrowed her eyes and swung the hockey stick at Jimmy's face, missing his nose by mere inches. "Drats...stay still!" she yelled and prepared for a second launch.

Jimmy drew his head back as far as he could and began to scoot away from Bonnie. "Get this insane woman away from me!" he shouted.

"Insane?" Bonnie screamed and lost her focus.

"Oh no," Sarah cried out. "Bonnie...no!"

Bonnie raised the hockey stick up into the air and prepared to start axing Jimmy in half. "I'll show you insane!" she yelled and brought the hockey stick down with all of her might.

Then Amanda leaped out and caught the hockey stick before it made contact with Jimmy's head. The hockey stick made an awful *Whack* sound on Amanda's hand. The poor woman let out a terrible howl, let go of the hockey stick, and began dancing around the storage room. "That smarts...oh that smarts...oh boy, oh boy, does that smart..."

Sarah snatched the hockey stick away from Bonnie. "Go make coffee."

Bonnie sighed. "I made a little mistake again, didn't I?"

"Yes, honey, you did," Sarah said in a clear voice. "Go back out front, okay?"

Bonnie bowed her head and left the storage room. But after a moment, the idea of brewing more coffee faded from her mind. Instead, she put on her muffler hat and quietly slipped out into the dark, snowy night. "I'm not good for anything or anyone...I'm just no good," she began to cry and ran off into the snow with her hands over her teary eyes.

Sarah threw the hockey stick down and checked on Amanda. "Are you okay, honey?"

Amanda held up the palms of her hands. "I think Bonnie broke my hands...I can't move them," she cried.

Sarah quickly examined Amanda's hands. "Honey, you're going to have some ugly bruises, but your hands aren't broken," she promised.

"That stupid ninny," Amanda snapped and then felt guilt

consume her heart. "Oh, I didn't mean that...I would never hurt Bonnie's feelings on purpose." Amanda checked her palms and then placed them into the pockets of her coat. "I know Bonnie doesn't mean any harm."

Sarah sighed and turned her attention back to Jimmy. "Look, pal, it's like this. Either help us or you're going to become a global target. You and I both know once I make your private text messages public you'll be marked. The senator will get rid of you so fast your head will spin."

Jimmy stared at Sarah. How in the world had he allowed a stupid, stupid, stupid...cop defeat him? Now he was a frog in a pot of water that had just been placed over a hot fire. "You're not going to let me go...what's the point?" he asked.

"The point is if I take Mooreland and Capps down, I can take Senator Kallerson down. You can turn state's evidence and get immunity...or maybe a reduced sentence. You should be okay in a federal prison," Sarah explained. "I'm sure a trained military solider like yourself will spend quite a lot of time and energy contemplating how to escape, too. I could be wrong?"

"Do you really think a loser cop like yourself—"

"Watch it, you filthy bloke," Amanda warned. "My hands may hurt but I can still slug you!"

Jimmy glared at Amanda. "Your friend is mistaken if she believes she's powerful enough to take down Mooreland and Capps. My job was..." Jimmy caught his mouth.

"Kill Mayor Mooreland and blame José's death on him? Yes, I know. I read your text messages." Sarah pulled Jimmy's cell phone out of her coat pocket. "Around the time you left the police station tonight, Senator Kallerson sent you a text...a change in plans, so to speak." Sarah brought up the text Senator Kallerson had sent Jimmy. "Kill Mooreland. Plant the evidence on him. Then we will take down Capps. Both men have betrayed me. Big meeting tonight."

Jimmy closed his eyes. If that text went public...his mind couldn't imagine the ramifications. Senator Kallerson's political enemies would rip the man's public and personal life to shreds and destroy anyone associated with him. On top of that, Jimmy clearly understood, Senator Kallerson's political enemies would use the Justice Department, the FBI, and the halls of Congress to attack him, too. Senator Kallerson would be destroyed, along with his associates, who were extremely powerful people within the European Union and the United Nations. Jimmy found it amazing how one text could cause a war...and end his life. "Kallerson isn't worth my life," he growled, snapped his eyes open, and looked at Sarah. "Big meeting tonight...maybe I can tell you more about that. We can help each other, right? Capps flew into town on his private jet for this meeting."

"In this weather?" Sarah asked.

"Yes, in this weather," Jimmy snapped. "I told you it was a big meeting. Mooreland and Capps are meeting with Edward Russel—"

"Edward Russel? The leader of Britain's United Central Party?" Amanda asked.

"You've heard of Edward Russel?" Jimmy asked.

"The name Edward Russel sickens every decent Brit," Amanda nearly gagged. "And if I'm not mistaken, and I know I'm not, Edward Russel's...gag and puke...brother is my country's representative to the United Nations."

"You're not as dumb as you look," Jimmy congratulated Amanda. "Now put two and two together and let your brain chew on some facts."

Amanda looked at Sarah with worried eyes. "Imagine a group of people trying to create a communist world on steroids, love," she explained. "We're talking about people who openly advocate population control...population reduction, to be more precise...controlled birth rates around the globe..." Amanda held up her injured hand and began to gently count on her fingers: "Indoctrination centers that will force every bloke on earth to obey one world government...a global system...food control...medicine and healthcare...education...family...church…freedom...all destroyed in the name of peace. We're talking about men who openly claim that billions of people need to be 'mercifully' sterilized in order to better mankind." Amanda felt a shiver run down her spine. "Soulless people, love."

"People who are making progress," Jimmy warned. "That's why I choose the winning side."

"Does it look like you're on the winning side now, you moron?" Amanda asked and threw her hands up into the air. "You're not very smart, are you?"

Sarah put a hand on Amanda's shoulder. "So Edward Russel is in town?"

"Yeah," Jimmy nodded, twisting his hands futilely inside the handcuffs holding him captive.

"Pete mentioned Edward Russel to me," Sarah told Amanda.

"Why didn't you tell me, love?"

Sarah sighed. "Sometimes a cop thinks about so much at once she forgets to get orange juice at the grocery store. I didn't think Russel was important, at the time." Sarah focused on Jimmy. "So there's some pretty big fish in town tonight. And your job was to kill Mooreland...but," Sarah paused and read a second text message. "Ignore last message. Had phone meeting. Kill Russel and Capps and pin the murders on Mooreland, per Houston Middleton."

Jimmy let out a heavy sigh. "Cop, you don't understand—"

"No, I think I do. I know that name quite well. Houston Middleton was Speaker of the House here in America, but he was publicly shamed and forced into retirement after facts were made public about shady construction deals with foreign companies. If I'm not mistaken, Houston Middleton used the Department of Federal Land Management to force people off their land in Idaho, Florida, Maine, California, New York, and Wyoming. I guess that man just doesn't give up the fight."

Jimmy let out a huff. "Middleton is still connected to the CIA. He has contacts...the man is more powerful now than he was when he was in office."

"Seems like he has enemies—" Sarah stopped talking when her cell phone rang. She quickly checked the call and saw Mike's number. "Yeah, Mike?" she answered the call.

The cold barrel of a gun pressed against the side of Mike's head. "Detective Spencer," he said as sweat poured down the side of his face, "stand down, do you hear me?"

Sarah heard anger and fear in Mike's voice. She closed her eyes and let out a horrible moan. "Mike, remain calm," she whispered. "I have a plan."

"Stand down and leave town at once," Mike ordered Sarah. "Detective Massio and I will be killed if you don't leave. You have one hour. Please—"

Mayor Mooreland snatched Mike's cell phone away. "Detective Spencer, this is the mayor speaking. I have no desire to fight with you. If you obey and do not bother me again, I will let you live. If you refuse, your husband…Conrad Spencer…will die. If that doesn't make you stand down, I will have Amanda Hardcastle killed, along with her husband who is currently visiting London. And if that isn't enough, I will make you watch, in person, the very painful, very cruel death of your dear friend Pete. You have one hour to leave town…and don't take the stool pigeon with you. Leave him, if you've got him tied up or whatever. I'll be expecting you to leave by the south county road. I'll be watching." And with those words, Mayor Mooreland ended the call, leaving Sarah frantic for a solution.

"My husband?" Amanda whispered to Sarah, having heard every word Mayor Mooreland had threatened. "Love…he's going to kill us? And my hubby…"

Sarah put her cell phone away and looked down at the floor. "It's not checkmate yet," she whispered, but deep down, she worried that the odds were finally against her.

"What are we going to do, love?" Amanda pleaded in a desperate voice tinted with anger and fear.

Sarah plopped down on a cardboard box, closed her eyes, and let her mind drift back to the old black man in Oregon. The old man stood in his antique kitchen, boiling a pot of beans on his old gas stove. *Got yourself in a mess, huh?* he asked Sarah and let out a little chuckle. He wiped a hand on his soft brown shirt and his blue overalls.

"What do I do?" Sarah asked, watching steam rise up from the boiling beans and cover the glass on the kitchen window. Sarah felt desperation gripping her. "I'm only one woman.

Even with Amanda, there is only so much we can do...we nearly died at the hot springs, for crying out loud!"

The old man picked up a wooden spoon and began to stir the beans. *Seems to me you still have a brain, right? If a person still has a brain in their head, then that means they're still mighty dangerous. Why, even a wounded dog can still bite.*

"I'm not a wounded dog," Sarah told the old man and continued to watch the steam from the boiling beans play in the kitchen air.

Oh, I wouldn't say that. But it seems to me you're always a wounded dog when it comes to these cases of murder. Yes sir, seems like you sure know how to keep biting at the hand that tries to put you in the grave, too. The old man turned and looked at Sarah with eyes that held an overpowering wisdom. *You're in a mess, but that don't mean you're in the grave, girl. You got a brain...which is your biting teeth...to think with. Don't go letting some mangy humans steal your food. No sir, you best growl those teeth and get to biting at their hands.*

"My brain is fresh out of ideas."

The old man returned his attention back to the boiling beans. *Water don't know it can make these beans turn soft until the fire underneath wakes it up. Seems to me you need a fire set under your brain.* The old man slowly put down the wooden spoon, reached out, took Sarah's hand and said in a stern but loving voice: *Play dead, girl, and let the beast sniff you...and then attack. But don't attack until the fire has warmed the water enough to boil the beans.* And with those words, the old man vanished before Sarah's eyes.

"Love?" Amanda asked, staring at Sarah's closed eyes. "Now isn't the time to nap."

Sarah popped her eyes open and looked at Jimmy. "Play dead," she whispered.

"What, love?" Amanda asked.

"You'll see, June Bug," Sarah answered in an urgent voice. She shot to her feet and walked over to Jimmy. "I'll make you a deal."

"What kind of deal?" Jimmy asked.

"I won't turn you over to Mayor Mooreland if you help me. All you have to do is talk into your cell phone. Easy enough," Sarah explained.

Jimmy studied Sarah's urgent eyes. What was the woman planning? He didn't know. All Jimmy did know was that Mayor Mooreland, Patrick Capps, and Edward Russel wanted him dead.

Sarah drew in a deep breath and looked at Amanda. "Mooreland and his gang of thugs have no intention of letting us live, June Bug. We know too much. He wants us out in the open...if we step one foot out of this toy store, we're dead."

"You're a smart cop," Jimmy told Sarah. "Capps and Russel are most likely standing at a distance. The pressure is on Mooreland to kill us. Capps and Russel wouldn't dare stain their hands...not at this point, I don't think." Jimmy studied the back door. "Mooreland still has Jack Mayes."

"Who?" Sarah asked.

Jimmy hesitated. "Jack Mayes," he told Sarah in a low voice. "Jack is Mooreland's secret ace."

"Stop talking in riddles, you bloody git!" Amanda yelled at Jimmy. "My hubby's life is in danger...Sarah's hubby's life is in danger...Pete..." Amanda shook her fist at Jimmy. "Talk straight or I'm going to slug you!"

"Jack Mayes is a private contractor. My boss. Jack hired me

to work for Mooreland, get it? All Mooreland has to do is pick up the phone and have Jack send in some more guys to kill us off. My guess is at least three to five trained assassins are en route to this town as we speak."

"How do you know Mooreland doesn't have a new team already set in place?" Sarah asked.

"We would already be dead if Jack Mayes had his guys in town," Jimmy assured Sarah. "That's why Mooreland gave you an hour to get lost. That's why he told you to take the south county road. Nothing but wilderness on that road. Perfect place for an ambush." Jimmy looked at Sarah. "You leave town, drive a few miles south, encounter some kind of roadblock...maybe a bunch of snow piled up on the road...I've seen him work like this before. He'll wait until you try to turn around and then it's lights out as the bullets start flying at you from both sides of the road."

"Which brings us back to my request," Sarah told Jimmy as her mind imagined the dark ambush before her eyes. She saw armed killers firing at a helpless SUV holding two frightened women with no place to run. No good. "I want Mooreland, Capps, Russell...all of these rotten men. And you're going to help me."

"You're dreaming, cop. It'll never work."

"Yes, it will," Sarah assured Jimmy. "Look, all you have to do is tell Mooreland you killed me and my friend and cut some kind of deal with him," Sarah explained. "You also have to get Mooreland to come to the toy store."

"Impossible."

"Is it?" Sarah asked Jimmy. "It's either play on my side or wait for Mooreland's hired killers to show up and finish you off. If you take my side, you face prison instead of the grave. If you take Mooreland's side...according to the look in your eyes...you'll be dead meat in the next hour or so."

Jimmy wiggled his wrist. There was no chance of escaping the handcuffs. To make matters worse, his right hand was crying out in pain...permanently disabled...and his right shoulder ached so bad that he could barely tolerate the pain. And it was the pain—the miserable taste of pain—forcing Jimmy to grow weaker by the second, mentally and physically. Surely, he thought, Mooreland's team of killers would make sure he suffered more pain before they killed him; hired killers enjoyed inflicting pain in their victims. "I'm not your friend, cop," he warned. "But..." Jimmy gritted his teeth, "I have a better chance to survive in prison...and if I live to see prison bars...and ever escape, which I will...I'll call it even with you. Deal?"

"Good enough," Sarah nodded. She quickly snatched Jimmy's cell phone out of her coat pocket. "June Bug, please go check on Bonnie."

Amanda hesitated. "Love, what's your plan?" she pleaded.

"We're all going to play dead," Sarah explained. "And when Mooreland arrives...we'll bite." Sarah walked over to Amanda, put a gentle hand on her shoulder, and said, "Think back to the hot springs, honey. Just like that."

Amanda felt a tear drop from her eye. "I guess so," she said and forced a brave smile to her shaky lips. "Being your best friend is never boring, love," she tried to joke. "Next time you visit a relative, leave me at home."

"Next time a relative calls me, I'm not going to answer the phone," Sarah struggled to joke back. Amanda smiled and hurried away to check on Bonnie. Sarah turned back to Jimmy, steadied her mind, and then used his cell phone to call

Mayor Mooreland. "Make it good," she begged Jimmy, placed the call on speaker, and stuck the phone close to Jimmy's mouth.

Mayor Mooreland answered with a cold voice. "One hour, Detective—"

"This is Jimmy," Jimmy stated in a stern, angry voice. "My task is complete. The three women are dead."

Mayor Mooreland walked over to a large stone fireplace, holding an expensive cigar in his wrinkled hand, and looked into a blazing fire. "Explain."

"I guess they thought handcuffs could hold me," Jimmy told Mayor Mooreland in a professional soldier's voice. "I had to wait until the cop looked away."

"I heard some very...disturbing information come from Detective Spencer's mouth, Jimmy, concerning...certain text messages sent to you from Kallerson."

"Yeah, yeah, so what?" Jimmy barked. "I'm not your best friend, Mooreland. I'm in this game for money. If I wanted you dead, you would be dead. I stay with the highest bidder. What's it to you if I'm scamming some extra cash from Kallerson?" Jimmy looked up at Sarah with fierce eyes. "Mooreland, they're dead. That's what you wanted, that's what you got."

Mayor Mooreland turned around and spotted two men wearing dark black suits standing in a fancy parlor, smoking cigars, and discussing the future of Four Ridges. Mike and Tony were also in the parlor, tied up and gagged. He smelled a rat. "I want proof."

"Come and see for yourself," Jimmy barked at Mooreland. "And bring my cash. I'm ending my contract tonight. I'm calling Jack now to tell him I want to be reassigned."

Mayor Mooreland rubbed his chin. Patrick Capps and Edward Russel, unaware that he was speaking with Jimmy, continued to discuss the implementation of their plans. The two men were calmly waiting for Jack Mayes's team of hired killers to arrive, fully expecting the lower man on the food chain—Mayor Mooreland—to clean up the mess while they kept their hands clean. Mayor Mooreland despised being the lower man on the food chain and slowly felt a strange—if not frightening—thought enter his mind. "Kill Capps and Russel...pin the murder on Jimmy...eliminate my enemies... make good with Kallerson and Middleton...perfect," he whispered.

"You there, Mooreland?" Jimmy snapped.

"I'm here," Mayor Mooreland promised and felt a hideous grin touch his evil face. He slowly reached into the inside pocket of his silver coat and removed a gun that had a silencer attached to the barrel. "Jimmy, perhaps I jumped to conclusions. You have been a faithful employee. I honestly can't see a man of your nature working for the likes of Kallerson." Mayor Mooreland glanced at Patrick Capps and Edward Russel with devious, deadly eyes. "Send me a photo of the dead women in the next ten minutes. If I'm satisfied, then I will travel to your location and pay you the money that is owed to you."

"What about Capps and Russel?"

"Oh, I wouldn't worry about them," Mayor Mooreland grinned. "My two dear friends will take the ride with me...one way or the other." Mayor Mooreland shifted his eyes to Mike and Tony. He would allow those two idiots to live. Why? Fear always destroyed a man—and controlled his heart. Mayor Mooreland had plans for Mike and Tony...at least until he had the town of Four Ridges under his complete control. "Ten minutes...send me those photos," he warned Jimmy, ended the call, and then, without any hesitation, walked into the parlor and shot Capps and Russel, ending the lives of two men who were planning to do the same to him. Betrayal and murder were all part of the game. Trust no one was the key to survival.

"You two," Mayor Mooreland told Mike and Tony as he put his gun away with a calm hand, "if you want to live, you will learn to obey me. Is that clear?"

Mike glanced over at Tony. Tony nearly peed his pants. Had he really seen the old man gun down two men? Mayor Mooreland was an old man...ready for a nursing home and fiber cereal...he wasn't a killer. Only, Tony had witnessed with his own eyes how a deadly wolf can wear sheep's clothing. "I want the town of Four Ridges under my complete power," Mayor Mooreland explained. "However, I have to play nice with Senator Kallerson first. The death of these two men will certainly put me on the senator's good side. That's where you two idiots will assist me. Your job will be to assure Senator Kallerson that you heard the two I killed speak a few lies, lies that I'm going to teach you. Is that clear?"

Mike looked at Tony again. Tony was staring up at Mayor Mooreland with shocked eyes. Oh boy, Mike thought, Tony was in a real bad state, which meant it was up to him to save the day. But how? His hands were tied up and his gun was...somewhere. How could a man in his position save the day?

What Mike didn't know was that Bonnie Malloy was on her way over to Mayor Mooreland's house. The upset woman was going to give the old man a piece of her mind. Bonnie Malloy's life had been turned upside down, and it was all

Mayor Mooreland's fault. "I'll tell that mayor a thing or two," Bonnie said, walking down a snowy, dark sidewalk with tears falling from her eyes. "I'll tell that mayor just how awful he is and then punch him square in the nose. That's what I'm going to do..." Bonnie wiped at her tears and continued toward Mayor Mooreland's house, ignoring the snow and cold, only focusing on the task at hand.

Chapter Fourteen

"She's gone!" Amanda burst into the storage room on frantic legs. "Love...Bonnie...I can't find her anywhere."

"Oh no," Sarah moaned, quickly put Jimmy's cell phone away, and looked at Amanda with worried eyes. "We have ten minutes to take a photo of three dead women."

Amanda stared at Sarah. "Three dead women?" she asked in a confused voice and then threw her hands up into the air. "This night just keeps filling with excitement, doesn't it?"

"You better find that fat whale or Mayor Mooreland will kill all of us," Jimmy warned.

Sarah locked her eyes on the back door. "What now?" she fretted, closed her eyes, and went back to the old black man in Oregon. Only this time the snowman blocked her path.

Chapter Fifteen

Amanda appeared dead. She lay on the floor, spread out across the chalk line like a rag doll, with a little blood—which was simply watered-down ketchup—soaking through the back of her dress in order to mimic a single gunshot wound. "Let's hope this works," Sarah said, snapped a photo of Amanda with Jimmy's cell phone, and then quickly helped Amanda stand up. "My turn…let's make it good."

Amanda quickly grabbed the cell phone as Sarah took a packet of ketchup out of her coat pocket. A little box of ketchup packets had been found under the front counter. Obviously, Bonnie liked ketchup and didn't approve of waste. "How's this?" Sarah asked, rubbing ketchup on her forehead and then using her finger to make what appeared to be a line of blood running down her face.

"Creepy," Amanda shivered.

Sarah reluctantly took her blonde bangs and mixed them in with the ketchup. Jimmy watched with curious eyes.

"Okay...let's take a photo." Sarah quickly lay down next to the back door, closed her eyes, and positioned her body in a way that resembled a woman who had been shot down while running for her life. Amanda felt a cold shiver run down her spine and then quickly—but very cautiously—captured a realistic photo of Sarah. "Okay, love, you're a star now."

"Great." Sarah flung her eyes open and stormed to her legs. She wiped the blood off her brow with a tissue. "Okay...now...let's see if this works."

"You're crazy, cop," Jimmy told Sarah.

Sarah ignored Jimmy's remark, grabbed an enormous teddy bear, covered it with a white tablecloth that she had found under some toys, and then doused the sheet with ketchup. "Okay, honey...snap a photo. We have..." Sarah checked her watch. "We have three minutes to spare."

Amanda drew in a worried breath and then approached the teddy bear. "Please let this work," she begged, snapped a photo of the faked homicide scene, and then handed Sarah the cell phone. "Okay, love, we're all set."

Sarah nodded and swiftly sent the photos to Mayor Mooreland's cell phone. "All we can do now is wait," she said and sat down on a pile of boxes. "Where can Bonnie be?" she asked and shook her head. "Why did she leave?"

"I guess we hurt her feelings," Amanda suggested in a sad voice. "The poor dear...she really means no harm, love. She's simply—"

"Different?" Sarah finished for Amanda.

"Yes, different," Amanda agreed, sat down on a wooden crate, and sighed. "Maybe it's better that Bonnie vanished on us, love? I mean, we're...what's the American word...oh yes, brawling with some pretty bad...uh...dudes."

Sarah looked into Amanda's sweet, scared face that was attempting to appear brave. "I love you, June Bug. No matter that happens tonight, I want you to know that I love you so very much." Sarah reached out and took Amanda's hand. "You've stood by me through thick and thin, the good and the bad...you're my everything, honey."

Amanda felt a tear drop from her pretty eye. "Don't talk like that, love," she begged. "This isn't the end for us. You're going to be a mother and...we're going to shop for baby clothes at O'Mally's, do you hear me?" Amanda wiped at her tear. "We're going to grow very old together, you and me, and we're going to make sure our hubbies grow old with us."

"I pray," Sarah whispered, fighting back her own tears. "June Bug, the snowman is never going to leave me alone until I kill it," she explained in a low whisper. "I keep having this feeling that somewhere...out there in the unknown...there's one last battle that has to happen...a showdown that has to take place...and the winner will either be me or the snowman. But until then I have to keep fighting my way through these dark alleys."

"Love," Amanda promised, "whatever the future holds, no matter how many dark alleys you have to face, I'll always be standing at your side." Amanda forced a weak smile to her face. "You know me...double-o Amanda Hardcastle at your service, ma'am."

"I like that," Sarah actually smiled. "I may make that woman into a new character in my next novel. Of course, I'll make her into the hero."

"I'm not a hero, love. As a matter of fact...I'm scared out of my wits right about now," Amanda confessed. "Who would have guessed that a woman like Bonnie Malloy would become tangled up in such a dangerous murder case like this...filled with all these horrible people?" Amanda stood up. "We're in small-town America, for crying out loud...goodness, we would be safer walking through the Bronx at midnight with signs on our back that read 'Free Cash.'"

"Yeah," Sarah agreed and then stopped when Jimmy's cell phone let out a chime that informed Sarah a text message had arrived. "Here we go," she said and quickly checked the text message. Amanda bit down on her lip and studied Sarah's eyes as she read the text message. Silence fell in the storage room. The sound of crying winds filled the void. Jimmy closed his eyes and waited. "He took the bait," Sarah announced and read the text message out loud. "Will be to your location in twenty minutes. Killed Capps and Russel. Your new job is to get rid of their bodies before you leave town."

Jimmy snapped his eyes open. "What?"

Sarah read the text message again.

"Hey, you have to set me free. Mooreland has gone insane...he's..." Jimmy shook his head. "Capps and Russel are connected to some very powerful people. Mooreland will cause a war."

"Maybe that's what the man wants?" Sarah suggested. She looked at Jimmy. "What does this mean?" she asked. "Will Mooreland still need Jack Mayes?"

"I doubt Mooreland even called Jack Mayes," Jimmy confessed. "He might have...I don't know. But if he killed Capps and Russel...it's possible he will call Jack Mayes and have the new team stand down."

Sarah felt a tinge of hope touch her heart. "Okay," she said and turned to Amanda. "Honey, get into the front room and hide in the dollhouse." Amanda looked at Sarah with caring, worried eyes and then hurried away. "Jimmy," Sarah explained, "I'm going to take the handcuffs off you. If you try to attack me...then so be it. I don't want to fight you and I'm sure you're ready to seek some medical attention for your hand and shoulder. We can either help each other or kill each other."

"What about José Lopez?" Jimmy asked. "You know I killed him."

"A woman has to pick her fights," Sarah told Jimmy. "Mooreland may be arriving with a hit team, who knows? He may be arriving alone...he may have killed Mike and Tony." Sarah stared at Jimmy with careful eyes. "Mooreland may have believed the photos I sent him or not," she finished, hoping Jimmy would buy her lie. "There comes a time when a cop has to make hard decisions."

"Take the cuffs off, then. I'm on your team...for now. But when this is over, I'm splitting, do you hear me? If you stand in my way, I'll kill you."

"Fair enough." Sarah, using extreme caution, removed the handcuffs and backed away to a safe distance. "Your job is to tell Mooreland you placed our bodies out in the snow and then get him to start talking. I'll be over there behind those boxes. I want Mooreland alive, okay?"

"And if Mooreland shows up with a hit team?" Jimmy asked and held out his good hand. "I need my gun."

Sarah bit down on her lip and then reached into her coat pocket, took out Jimmy's gun, and slid it across the floor. "Use your wounded hand to convince Mooreland we had a fun fight."

Jimmy picked up his gun, thought about taking a shot at Sarah, and then backed down. The stakes were too high now, and Mooreland had to be his target. He would handle Sarah later. However…if Mooreland had killed Capps and Russel, that was bad news...but if he killed Mooreland in return, Senator Kallerson would certainly advance his position in the game. "Get out of sight, cop."

Sarah nodded and hid behind a stack of boxes and waited for Mayor Mooreland to arrive. Jimmy sat down on a wooden crate, checked his wounded hand, and began to form a plan, not realizing that Sarah was one step ahead of him. What Jimmy—and Mayor Mooreland—didn't know was that Amanda had slipped outside into the snow instead of hiding in the massive dollhouse. Amanda Hardcastle was on a mission. "Stay calm," Sarah whispered and waited. Ten minutes later, a hard knock struck the back door.

"Password?" Jimmy grunted in an undertone.

"Solid grounds," a bitter voice called out.

Jimmy checked his wounded hand, examined his wounded shoulder, and then walked over to the back door. "Are you alone?" he demanded.

"I'm alone," Mayor Mooreland assured Jimmy.

Jimmy stepped away from the door, threw on his night vision goggles, turned off the lights, and then said, "Door's unlocked. Enter."

Mayor Mooreland, unaware that Amanda was watching him from behind a large, snow-soaked tree, opened the back door. Amanda quickly sent Sarah a text message. "The bloke is alone."

Sarah shielded her cell phone and read the text message as Mayor Mooreland opened the back door. "Turn on the lights," he demanded.

Jimmy ran to Mayor Mooreland through the darkness, grabbed the old man, pushed him outside, and searched the surrounding area. All was clear. "Inside," he barked, yanked Mayor Mooreland back inside, threw him into a corner and then turned on the lights. "Did you really kill Capps and Russel?" he demanded.

Mayor Mooreland rubbed his left wrist as Jimmy took off his night vision goggles and tossed on his eyeglasses. "You can become a part of something great," he replied in a calm voice.

Jimmy stared at Mayor Mooreland and investigated the man's eyes. "You did kill them...are you insane? There will be retaliation...Kallerson and Middleton will be forced to act. There will be a war."

"Will there?" Mayor Mooreland asked. "Perhaps if I convince Kallerson that I'm now on his side, a war will not be necessary. After all, we are both aware that Russel was attempting to manipulate Kallerson and Middleton. Kallerson will be pleased that I killed his enemies." Mayor Mooreland glanced down at Jimmy's wounded hand. "It's all about power and control, is it not?" he asked and then searched the storage room. "Where are the bodies?"

"Out in the snow," Jimmy explained and held up his wounded hand. "The stupid cop and I had an unpleasant meeting. She managed to get off two shots at me before I put her down..." Jimmy sounded extremely convincing—so convincing that Mayor Mooreland, who never believed a word anyone said, actually believed him.

"I'm sorry to see you in such pain."

"Look, forget about my hand," Jimmy snapped. "I want payment and then I'm leaving town. I'll call Jack Mayes and request a new assignment. Jack will send you a new man in my place."

"Of course," Mayor Mooreland nodded. "I have your

money in my office. Shall we?" Mayor Mooreland turned toward the back door. As he did, he slid his hand into his coat pocket and, without any warning, turned around with a gun in his hand, prepared to shoot Jimmy dead. Jimmy fired. Only his gun went *Click*. Mayor Mooreland grinned, aimed his gun straight at Jimmy's chest, and began to squeeze the trigger. As he did, the sound of a gun went off. A bullet tore through the air and struck Mayor Mooreland in his right hand. Mayor Mooreland let out a loud cry, dropped his gun, and stumbled back toward the back door.

"Hands in the air!" Sarah yelled at Jimmy. "Now!"

Jimmy narrowed his eyes. "You tricked me you...stupid cop!"

Sarah reached into her coat pocket, yanked out a pair of handcuffs, and threw them at Jimmy. "Put them on."

Jimmy snarled at Sarah, ignored her command, and made a mad dash toward the back door. He was met by a very angry Amanda who put a bullet in his right leg. Jimmy dropped down into the snow and began yelling in rage. "I guess this little English crumpet isn't so stupid after all," Amanda told Jimmy and raised her face up into the falling snow, closed her eyes, and let out a deep breath. "Remind me to stay home from now on."

Sarah walked over to Mayor Mooreland, grabbed the old man, and shoved him out into the snow. "You're both going to prison," she explained, trying to sound tough, but she ended up sounding plum exhausted. She looked at Amanda through the falling snow and smiled. "I guess the bad guys helped us by killing each other."

Amanda rolled her eyes. "Silly blokes...enough to make a woman wonder how they even wipe their own rear ends."

Deep down, Amanda was grateful that in the end, evil betrayed itself, as it always seemed to do. "Can we go home now?"

"Not yet," a harsh voice said.

Sarah and Amanda spun around and saw a man step out of the dark snow and walk forward. "Freeze!" Sarah screamed.

"Put your gun down, Detective Spencer," Houston Middleton ordered. "Look at your friend."

Sarah looked at Amanda and saw three red dots on her face—snipers were trained on her at that very moment. "No..."

Houston Middleton eased forward on calm feet, keeping his eyes hidden under a gray fedora hat. "Mooreland, tonight you accomplished my goal through the avenues of betrayal. I am very pleased that you killed Capps and Russel for me."

"I didn't do so good, boss," Jimmy moaned. "I took three bullets."

"You convinced Kallerson to trust you and captured some very damaging text messages he sent you," Middleton congratulated Jimmy. "I will deal with Kallerson at a later time. Right now, I have the man I want."

"Don't kill me," Mayor Mooreland began to beg for his life. "I killed Capps and Russel. I—"

Houston Middleton raised his right hand up into the air. Four men dressed in black military uniforms appeared out of the snowy darkness. Two of the men grabbed Jimmy and the last two snatched Mayor Mooreland and dragged him away. "Go back to Snow Falls, Alaska, Detective Spencer," he warned Sarah. "My fight isn't with you. Forget everything that has happened tonight, or you will become my enemy. Let's not let it come to that." Houston Middleton walked off into the darkness and vanished. As he did, the beams of red light dancing across Amanda's face vanished.

Sarah grabbed Amanda, pulled her inside the storage room, closed and locked the back door, and then hugged the woman as tight as she possibly could. Amanda hugged Sarah back. "Let's go home, honey," Sarah whispered. "This case is over."

"Boy, tell me about it," Amanda sighed, looked Sarah in her eyes, and simply shook her head. "Makes you feel like a little fish in a big ocean filled with sharks, doesn't it? There we were, thinking we created a brilliant plan and we were being watched the entire time...everyone was being watched by the big shark."

Sarah sighed, looked at the back door, and shook her head. "Pete has the right idea," she said and then felt a shaky laugh leave her mouth. "Sure, Los Angeles has crime, but nothing like small-town America."

Amanda took Sarah's hand. "Come on, let's get out of here—"

Sarah's cell phone interrupted Amanda. Sarah checked the call and saw Mike's cell phone number appear. "Mike?" she answered in a quick voice.

"No, it's Bonnie," Bonnie told Sarah in a furious voice. "Cousin Sarah, you better get over to the mayor's house. Chief Early is going to arrest me...I kinda lost my temper and knocked Tony Massio out cold again. But golly, it wasn't my fault. I found Chief Early and Tony all tied up in the mayor's parlor. All I did was untie them and then Tony ran his mouth and called me stupid for leaving the toy store...sorry, Cousin Sarah."

Sarah heard Mike yelling in the background. She closed

her eyes and sighed. "Tell Mike everything is clear on our end and that we'll meet him at the police station...with bail."

Amanda grinned. "Well, at least now we know where Bonnie is," she told Sarah and then walked away, shaking her head.

Chapter Sixteen

Bonnie giggled as she hurried to bring a plate of freshly baked banana nut muffins to the kitchen table in her warm kitchen. "Oh, this is so exciting," she told Sarah and Amanda. "I'm so excited you girls decided to stay on for a few days."

Sarah sat down at the kitchen table and smoothed down her deep green dress. "Cousin Bonnie, we decided to stay on because Chief Early is making me work Tony's shifts until Tony gets out of the hospital. You really knocked him for a loop."

Amanda grabbed a muffin and quickly dunked it into a cup of delicious hot chocolate. "At least we're getting free meals at the diner," she beamed. "And look at it this way, love…Conrad thinks we solved a simple murder case, my hubby thinks we solved a simple murder case, and no one is the wiser to what really took place in this little town."

Sarah grabbed a muffin, said a prayer of thanks, and took a bite. "I guess," she nodded and then looked at Bonnie. Poor Bonnie was wearing a bright pink sweater with red and green lipstick kisses printed all over it. The woman looked like a silly clown...but so sweet. "Well, Bonnie, it looks like your town had the trash taken out and should be getting back to normal."

"I know," Bonnie clapped her hands together. "And just think, the new mayor is going to tear down the town hall next to my toy store and go back to operating out of the old town hall. Oh, it'll be just like the old days. I'll have no neighbors and be able to play my toy store music as loud as I want." Bonnie clapped her hands together again.

Sarah took another bite of her muffin. As Bonnie celebrated, she thought about Tony Massio, Mac Newman, Mayor Mooreland, Jimmy Leque, Senator Kallerson, Patrick Capps, Edward Russel and Houston Middleton. A lot of big fish fighting it out in a small town in northern Michigan. One team struggling to have power and control over another team...one man's ideas fighting to overpower the ideas and principals America was founded on...so many different players but all with the same objective: destroy truth and freedom and create a system of power and control. That's what it really boiled down to, Sarah thought. Through all the twists and turns and backstabbing, the final answer was simple: power and control. Corrupt men—and women—fighting to control a world that was too divided to ever be whole again; and the battleground was a country that still flew the American flag. "I better get down to the police station and start my shift," Sarah said, finished off her muffin, and stood up. "Honey, are you going to help Cousin Bonnie at the toy store today?"

"No way," Amanda beamed. "Bonnie and I are going shopping."

"We sure are," Bonnie clapped her hands. "Amanda thinks my wardrobe needs a little...updating. Is that the word you used, sweetie?" Amanda smiled and nodded. Bonnie clapped her hands again. "I want to look really nice for my date with Tony."

"What?" Sarah gasped. "You're...Tony...you two are going on a date?"

Bonnie blushed. "My sweet Italian violin may play harsh music with his mouth, but his heart plays music that captures my love."

"Oh brother," Sarah said and rolled her eyes. "Cousin Bonnie, Tony is in the hospital because of you."

"I know. Isn't it romantic," Bonnie sighed with dreamy eyes.

"You deal with her," Sarah told Amanda, overwhelmed. She grabbed her coat and hurried out into a gentle falling snow.

"Detective Spencer," a voice said.

Sarah spun around and saw Houston Middleton leaning against the corner of the garage smoking a cigar. "It's nice to see you again."

Sarah began to go for her gun but thought better of it. "What do you want, Mr. Middleton?" she asked, forcing her voice to remain calm. "I'm only in town to—"

"To cover for Detective Massio until he recovers. Yes, I know," Houston Middleton told Sarah. He stepped away from the garage, tossed his cigar down into the snow, and then reached into a gray trench coat and pulled out a brown envelope. "Detective Spencer, regardless of what you heard about me, I am not a bad guy. In fact," Houston Middleton informed Sarah in a voice that made Sarah almost feel at ease, "I'm someone who cares about America."

"Do you?" Sarah asked.

Houston Middleton motioned around at the gentle falling snow. "Detective Spencer, the Revolutionary War never ended," he explained. "America is constantly at war...on the inside, within her heart. America is constantly being attacked by foreign enemies. Why do you think the United Nations is located in New York?" Houston Middleton looked at Sarah and allowed the falling snow to cover his fedora hat. "I'm a small fish, Detective Spencer. We all are, compared to the big picture."

"What is the big picture?"

Houston Middleton nodded toward the road. "Let's take a walk," he said. Sarah hesitated and then agreed. Houston Middleton walked Sarah down to the street and then turned north onto a snowy sidewalk. "Detective Spencer," he continued, "the big picture is ensuring that the constitution remains alive for centuries to come...to ensure our republic withstands the storms that are battering her shores."

Sarah kept her eyes forward. "You came back to tell me that?" she asked as falling snow landed on her lovely face.

"I'm a sixty-eight-year-old man, Detective Spencer," Houston Middleton explained. "My father has been in this battle since Roosevelt. When Kennedy was killed, the battle entered a new stage. Johnson was placed in power and used to disable America while dividing her people. From there, well...you have eyes. You see the state America is in, Detective Spencer." Houston Middleton stopped walking and looked at Sarah. "The madmen are in the halls of Congress, but they also walk the streets of every town in America freely. I handle one war and you handle another."

Sarah stared into Houston Middleton's eyes. "What do you want with me?"

"I want you to join my team, Detective Spencer," Houston Middleton explained and handed Sarah the brown envelope. "I am very impressed with your skills. Perhaps it's time to start fighting the real killers?"

Sarah studied the brown envelope and decided to open it. She saw cash, a plane ticket, and a new identification card with her own picture on it. "Mr. Middleton," she said and politely handed back the brown envelope, "I am fighting the real killers. Perhaps José Lopez wasn't an honorable man...or maybe he was, but the man was killed unjustly and you're protecting the person who killed him. I don't call that American justice. I call that a perversion of justice."

"Jimmy Leque is...was a valuable member of my team," Houston Middleton explained. "He was simply following orders. I didn't order him to kill an innocent man—"

"Enough...please," Sarah demanded. "Mr. Middleton, it's clear to me that there are many undercover players in your game, and I accept the fact that the values of our once great country are under attack. I'm aware of the mental and spiritual state of degradation that the American public has fallen into...chaos and insanity. I care for America and love her. However, the only difference is I'm not willing to become what our enemies are."

"Then you lose the battle," Houston Middleton informed Sarah in a stern tone. "Detective Spencer, there will always be necessary casualties in a war and if we don't attack our enemy on their level the real causalities will end up being those who love our country. I'm afraid real casualties are currently taking place as we speak."

"José Lopez was a real casualty."

Houston Middleton studied Sarah's eyes. "Detective

Spencer, you must be aware that the police force in our country was created to control the masses, not protect them. There are people who walk the halls of Congress that use the laws you uphold to destroy people. Do you honestly believe the life of José Lopez is worth losing a war over?"

"Mr. Middleton, when a person stops caring about justice for one single person...the war is already lost." Sarah looked out at the snow. "Good morning, Mr. Middleton. And goodbye."

Houston Middleton stared into Sarah's beautiful face and then simply walked away and never bothered her ever again. Sarah watched the man vanish down the snowy sidewalk and then walked back to the rental SUV parked in Bonnie's driveway and began to get in. Then she paused, looked out at the lovely falling snow, and closed her eyes.

Ain't easy, is it? the old black man asked Sarah, sitting on a long, wooden front porch staring off at a field covered with pumpkins. *No, sir, never is easy when it comes to life. First you have to figure your own mind out and then figure out everyone else.* The old man let out a chuckle, pulled an apple out of the pocket of his overalls, and took a bite. *That cousin of yours sure ain't easy to figure out. No, sir.*

Sarah sat down in a rocking chair, folded her hands together, and rested her mind. "I did want justice for José Lopez. The man was murdered, and justice needed to be served. I failed, I guess...but at least I tried."

You sure did try, and you did good.

"I had to figure out what to do."

You just had to figure out your mind was all. You see, you want a baby so bad that you started to put that want above everything else. Now, I'm not saying that's bad, but you got a monster chasing you, girl. You can't rest until that monster is dead.

"I'm too tired to fight the snowman anymore. You saw me...I'm getting weaker and weaker."

Weaker? Why, you managed to disable a hired killer.

"After you told me to stop being careful."

All I meant was that you had to stop twisting your mind into knots, girl. You had to stop worrying so much about not getting all scratched up. Cops get scratched up. It's part of who they are.

Sarah sighed, looked into the face of the sweet old man, found comfort, and then looked out at the pumpkins. "I began this case with the mind of a detective but ended it with the mind of a woman who just wants peace." The old man frowned.

Ain't never going to be any peace until the snowman is dead. That monster arrived in Alaska when that crazy model drifted in with the snow. No, sir. That snowman ain't going nowhere, girl. You're gonna have to kill it or it's gonna kill you.

"I know," Sarah whispered in a miserable voice. Then she felt a hand touch her shoulder.

Her eyes flew open and she saw Amanda looking at her. "June Bug?"

"Tony just called. He was released from the hospital an hour ago. We can go home now," Amanda smiled. "After we take Bonnie shopping first, of course."

Sarah looked deeply into Amanda's eyes. It was a woman like Amanda who kept her fighting.

Go on and rest for a bit, the old man told Sarah in a distant voice. *That snowman is out there somewhere but he ain't gonna attack again for a while. You best rest up and get ready.*

"Go inside and get Bonnie, honey," Sarah told Amanda,

relieved that Tony was out of the hospital. "We'll take her shopping and then drive back to Alaska where we belong." Amanda smiled, patted Sarah's hand, and hurried back inside.

Run…run… Sarah heard the snowman hiss in her ears *You will never get far, Sarah…oh no…because I have a little surprise waiting for you.* The snowman appeared before Sarah's eyes chewing on a candy cane and wearing a black leather jacket. *The Back Alley Killer isn't dead, Sarah…you know that. The killer has a daughter…it's time to get back into the dark alleys…oh yes.* The snowman tipped back its head and laughed a horrible laugh and then vanished.

Best rest up, the old black man warned Sarah, *'cause you got some fighting to do.*

Sarah lowered her gloved hand, felt her tummy, and whispered, "We'll be together soon, mommy promises…but first she has to make it safe for you…safe for all of us."

Sarah opened her eyes, watched the snow fall, and then called Conrad. Conrad was just about to call Sarah. He had great news. But, he told Sarah, he wouldn't reveal what the great news was until Sarah arrived back home. All Conrad confessed was that the news involved a baby.

About Wendy Meadows

Wendy Meadows, a USA Today bestselling author, delights readers with her engaging stories about women sleuths. She has penned numerous books, including the beloved Sweetfern Harbor, Sweet Peach Bakery, and Alaska Cozy series. Wendy calls New Hampshire home, where she lives with her husband, two sons, two mini pigs who have big personalities, and an adorable Labradoodle who rules the roost.

Visit her website at www.wendymeadows.com for latest releases, discounts and more!

amazon.com/author/wendymeadows

bookbub.com/profile/wendy-meadows

goodreads.com/wendymeadows

www.ingramcontent.com/pod-product-compliance
Lightning Source LLC
Chambersburg PA
CBHW071433130726
47997CB00006B/2065